cicada summer

'Makes you believe anything is possible.
My skin prickled, my pulse raced and I couldn't
put the book down until I'd finished.' Glenda Millard

'A treasure of a story, a story to slip into your
pocket like a feather or a perfectly round stone
—for keeps.' Penni Russon

c i c a d a
s u m m e r

kate
constable

ALLEN&UNWIN

To Jan and Bill, with love

First published in 2009

Allen & Unwin
83 Alexander St
Crows Nest NSW 2065
Australia
Phone: (61 2) 8425 0100
Fax: (61 2) 9906 2218
Email: info@allenandunwin.com
Web: www.allenandunwin.com

National Library of Australia
Cataloguing-in-Publication entry:

  Constable, Kate, 1966–   .
  Cicada summer/Kate Constable.
  9781741758283 (pbk.)

A823.4

Cover and text design by Design by Committee
Cover illustration by Ali Durham
Set in 12/17 pt Baskerville by Midland Typesetters, Australia
Printed in Australia by McPherson's Printing Group

9 8 7 6 5 4 3 2 1

1

Eloise floated on a sea of red and orange swirls. Dazzling golden threads shimmered through the cloth, the tiny fish embroidered on Mum's favourite skirt. Mum's arms were around her and Mum was singing softly.

. . . and little fishes, way down below, wiggle their tails, and away they go . . .

She was falling asleep on Mum's lap, safe and warm, wrapped in the billows of her skirt. The red and gold and purple of memory enfolded her and floated her away.

'Wake up, El for Leather!'

Eloise's eyes sprung open, and she struggled upright. A sheet of white light flashed from the rear window of the car in front, blinding her. She shut her eyes again and watched a dark shape drift down the inside of her eyelids, then jump up again, over and over, endlessly receding but never quite fading away.

Mum.

'Can't dream your whole life away!' cried Dad. 'You're not a little girl any more. High school next year. This is a fresh start, a fresh start for both of us. You can't move forward if you're always looking back . . .'

Eloise gazed at the passing landscape: parched paddocks, a harsh blue sky, dead trees. She shrank from it. Inside the car it was cool, but outside it was shimmering hot.

'Hel-lo, dreamy? Did you hear a word I said, El Dorado? Do you even know where we're going?'

Of course she knew. They were moving to the country, to the town of Turner where Dad grew up. He was building a convention centre; or maybe it was a hotel? It was hard to keep up with all his plans. There had been so many of them in the last couple of years, and they changed so quickly.

Eloise's grandmother Mo lived in Turner, she knew that much, though she couldn't remember meeting her. Mo and Dad had had a big fight years ago. And then she hadn't come to Mum's funeral, Dad had been so angry about that.

Eloise tried not to think about the funeral. She tried not to think about Mum. The red and golden swirls of Mum's skirt, the whisper of Mum's voice in her ear . . .

Eloise dropped a thick black curtain down on all those thoughts and smothered them.

Dad was humming along to the radio, tapping his hands on the wheel. He broke off to glance across at Eloise. 'Everything's going to work out perfectly this time. We'll settle down for good. This town's *ripe* for a convention centre . . .' And he was off again at top speed.

But it didn't matter if Eloise was convinced or not. Dad would do what he wanted anyway, like he always did. Since Mum died, Dad had quit jobs, moved cities, found girlfriends and left them. Bree was the latest; she and Dad had had a big fight last week. Dad had dragged Eloise out of bed and they'd gone to a hotel. Then he'd sweet-talked away five years of not speaking to Mo, and now they were going to visit her.

Eloise watched as the road signs beside the highway counted down the kilometres to Turner: 42, 29, 17, 8. Then all at once they were there, crawling down the main street. A line of trees marched along the middle of the road, casting black bars of shadow on the tarmac. A stone soldier leaned on his gun and gazed off across hills baked yellow in the sun.

'Still pretty,' said Dad. 'Even prettier once it gets a drop of rain. There's the river, the hills, the national park. Look at the shops. How's that for picturesque? And only—' Dad glanced at his watch. 'Only two hours from the city, give or take. Perfect for conferences, team-building weekends, you name it; they'll come rolling in.' He cocked his head toward Eloise. 'What do you say, Ella Fitzgerald, should we go and take a look at the building site? Mo's expecting us for lunch, but I never said it'd be an *early* lunch. And it's not like she's got anything to rush off to.'

Eloise was relieved. She wanted to put off meeting Mo as long as possible.

Dad swung the car off the main street and up a side road with a red-brick church at the top of a hill. 'Besides, knowing Mo, she'll have a million questions, and I don't know about you, but I'm not in the mood for an interrogation. Not today, not today,' he sang. 'Don't frighten me away, or I won't want to stay; don't ask me any questions today . . . Left at the church, then third turn on the right, if memory serves.'

Eloise counted the turn-offs as they passed. The dusty road dipped and rose between dry fields dotted with black and white cows.

'Here it is. The human compass strikes again!'

With a triumphant flourish, Dad steered the red sports car between a pair of sagging iron gates hung with a sign: PRIVATE PROPERTY. NO TRESPASSERS.

They bumped down a rutted driveway shaded with pine trees, a murky tunnel carpeted with brown needles. A tangle of overgrown trees and bushes rose before them as the car jolted around a curve and out onto a wide gravel drive splotched with weeds.

Dad switched off the engine and there was a sudden silence. 'There it is.'

It was a house. Eloise hadn't known there was a *house*.

She stepped out of the car into the heat, and stared. She'd never seen a house like this before. It was made of concrete, with wide windows and rounded corners, and balconies with slim iron railings. It looked more like a small ocean liner than a house; there were even round porthole windows. The shabby once-white walls were stained with green and streaked with rust. A double set of curved steps swerved apart then swooped together to meet at the double front doors.

'Art Deco, 1931.' Dad pointed to a pattern of stiff sculpted zigzags and wave shapes moulded to the wall. 'House looks like a flaming Christmas cake. But the land – the *land's* worth a fortune.'

He snapped open his mobile phone and began to take photos of the garden. He backed away round the side of the building, holding the phone out in front of him. Eloise watched him disappear, then, slowly, she climbed the steps to the front door. Two long glass panels ran down either side of it, etched with patterns of diagonal lines and triangles that weaved over and under.

Eloise turned and gazed out over the garden. It was as big as a park, but all tangled and neglected; weeds swarmed everywhere and the trees crowded round the house as if they were trying to press their way inside. A warm wind blew through Eloise's hair and her scalp prickled. She swung round sharply, but no one was there.

'Hey, Elastic Band!' Dad called from the rear of the house, and Eloise went to find him.

A paved terrace laced with dandelions ran along the back of the house; big windows and glass doors overlooked a gentle slope overgrown with yellow grass. Plywood was nailed across one smashed window. At the far end of the terrace was a covered porch, where Dad stood beside an open door.

'Human compass, human key.' Dad rubbed his shoulder. 'Is there anything this man can't do? Want to take a look inside?'

Eloise hung back. The inside of the house looked dark and creepy.

'Come on. You're not scared, are you?' Dad wiggled his fingers and *woooed* like a ghost. He laughed uneasily and wiped his forehead with his arm. 'Come on, Elementary. Chop chop. I'll be right behind you.'

Reluctantly Eloise stepped over the threshold.

She walked into a back passageway with rooms opening off on either side. The air was cool and stale and still. The rooms were shadowy, dim and green – an underwater kind of light – and there was a pungent musty smell.

Dad sniffed. 'Mice.'

Eloise took a hasty step backward, but Dad prodded her on.

'Not scared of a wittle mousie, are you? All old houses have mice . . . My convention centre won't have mice, I can promise you that.' Dad laughed suddenly and spread his arms wide. 'I've always wanted to get my hands on this place! I can do anything now – I could open a damn *zoo* if I felt like it! That idiot Mitchell, flaming Bree, think I can't *follow through*. I'll show 'em. Everything's going to change now, Elbow Grease, you know that, don't you? *This* time it's going to work out . . .'

His voice trailed away and he gazed into space, as if he could see the future unfolding before his eyes.

Eloise stepped deeper into the dimness. A ceaseless rustle of leaves, like scraps of paper tossed by the hot wind, whispered from the distant garden. A cicada started up somewhere near the porch.

At the end of the passage, Eloise pushed through a door covered in moth-eaten green felt and found herself in the grand foyer by the front door. A wide white staircase circled up to the next floor, and a round gallery looked down over the entrance hall. Eloise glimpsed big empty rooms opening out, one into another, like the chambers of a seashell. The black and white tiles and the zigzag patterns around the edges of the floor were furry with dust, and so were the stiff scalloped wave-shapes and zigzags moulded into the ceiling. Cobwebs drooped from the iron stair-railings.

As Eloise neared the front doors, the sun shifted and blazed through the glass panels, lighting the floor with a pattern of lines and angles. Eloise reached out and caught a tiny triangle of light in the palm of her hand.

Then the sun faded, and the foyer became a cave of shifting shadows. All the noises faded too – her father's muffled footsteps, the restless wind – and Eloise stood in a pool of silence.

Something flickered at the top of the stairs.

The back of Eloise's neck went cold. She wanted to run, but she couldn't move. She heard a voice call, *I'm coming!*, and a girl in a pale dress and a big sunhat came running down the stairs, her fingertips slipping down the curve of the slim iron railing.

Eloise couldn't breathe, her mouth was dry. She couldn't even run away.

But at the bottom of the steps, the girl in the pale dress faltered and stopped. For a fraction of a second she stood motionless, as if she were listening, then all at once she turned and stared straight at Eloise.

Their eyes met. Eloise tried to swallow; she backed away, one step, then another. And suddenly the foyer was empty. The ghostly girl was gone.

All the sounds came rushing back to full volume: the sighs and whispers of the garden, the shrill of cicadas, creaks and slams from the kitchen, Dad's brisk boots stomping up behind her. 'There you are, Elephant! What's up? Did a mouse run over your foot?'

Eloise managed to shake her head.

'So what do you reckon? Bit dark and stinky, isn't it. Paradise for the mice! Can you believe we've been here for an hour? Time ran away on me. We'd better head off; we're late for Mo. Better not make her cranky. You know this was her place, don't you? She hasn't lived here for years though – obviously. All mine now.' Dad grinned. 'Very generous of her to sign it over, so make sure you look grateful,

El's Bells. Of course, it's way too big for her to manage, and it would have been mine sooner or later anyway. Family property. And we're the only family, you and me, so—'

Dad kept talking all the way back to the car, but Eloise hardly heard him. She felt dizzy. She buckled her seatbelt as Dad spun the car around with a spray of gravel. Her head was turned toward the window but all she could see was the figure of the ghostly girl. Like a video replaying in her mind, she saw the girl run down the stairs, stop and turn to stare at Eloise. Run, stop, turn – over and over. Eloise shivered. She wished she could sit somewhere with her pencils and paper and draw what she'd seen. Already the picture in her mind had begun to waver and blur. Drawing it would fix it, pin it down. She shut her eyes and tried to print the memory on the inside of her eyelids.

'Great location, heaps of potential.' Dad was still talking. 'Don't know if it's worth trying to keep any of the garden in this drought. It looks half-dead already. But we'll see. Just you wait, Electric Chair. It's going to be magnificent.'

Eloise nodded, but Dad wasn't looking. A shiver ran through her and she hugged herself. She twisted her head to catch one last glimpse of the pale shape of the house, gradually swallowed up by the trees; like a ship slowly sinking beneath the waves.

2

'Here we are.' Dad pulled into Mo's driveway. He parked in front of the garage and switched off the engine, but then he just sat there; he didn't get out of the car.

The small house where Mo lived couldn't have been more different from the big white dilapidated mansion they'd just left behind. It was dark and low-roofed, hunched close to the ground. Faded striped awnings were lowered over the windows. The house seemed to scowl at the ground. Instead of neat beds of roses and azaleas, like most of the neighbours, Mo's yard was crammed with prickly native bushes. The neighbours' squares of lawn were all dead from the drought, but these prickly bushes struggled on.

The front door slowly opened. Eloise could just see a dark shape behind the screen door. A voice called out sharply from inside the house, 'You took your time! I was expecting you at one; it's nearly half-past two.'

'That's a fine greeting for the prodigal son.' Dad slammed the car door and glared toward the invisible figure. 'Come on, Elf Ears, she won't bite.'

Eloise slipped out of the car and followed Dad inside. Mo stepped back just far enough to let them in and then shut the door. She stood in the middle of the hallway with her fists on her hips. There was nothing ghostly about Mo. Her grey, wiry hair stood out in tufts like steel wool, and her eyes glittered suspiciously in her gaunt, bony face. One pair of glasses dangled round her neck, and another was shoved up on top of her wild tangle of hair. She wore a striped apron with a mud-coloured shirt and trousers underneath. Eloise's eyes went wide. Mo was clutching a knife, and her hands dripped with blood.

'Don't *flinch*. What are you, a kitten? It's only beetroot. Am I going to get a kiss from my only grandchild? Come on, get it over with. Save us, you're not some kind of shrinking violet, are you?'

Mo rammed on her glasses and peered sharply at Eloise.

'She's a bit shy, that's all. She's fine once she warms up, aren't you, Elevator Music?' Dad put his arm round Eloise's shoulders; he sounded so easy and confident that for a second Eloise almost believed it too.

Mo sniffed, testing the tip of the knife on her finger. 'She's a shrimp of a thing, isn't she? Looks more like ten than— How old are you now? Twelve, thirteen? Inherited the McCredie hair, poor kid. Got her mother's eyes though.' There was a pause, then Mo said, 'Sorry I couldn't make it to the funeral.'

Dad's arm tightened around Eloise. He didn't like talking about Mum. 'That's all water under the bridge now. What's done is done. Time to move on.' There was another pause. 'Sorry we're late. Stopped to have a look at the property.'

Mo sniffed again. 'Hope it lived up to expectations.'

'It's a fantastic piece of real estate. Pity the house is such an eyesore.'

Mo bristled for a second, then she looked away. 'Not my problem any more,' she said brusquely.

'All yours. Best thing I've ever done, get rid of that old place. And all its ghosts.'

Eloise jumped.

'Speaking metaphorically, of course.' Mo turned to her. 'Hungry? Like beetroot?'

After a second Eloise nodded. Her heart thudded, then slowed. Mo couldn't know what she'd seen at the house, could she?

'Cat got your tongue? She can speak, can't she, Stephen?'

'Of course she can. Could we move out of the doorway, do you think? Or would you prefer we got back in the car?'

'No need to get your knickers in a knot,' snapped Mo, and moved down the hallway. Bright purple-red spots had dripped all over the floor. Mo pointed down the corridor with a gory hand. 'Dining room. That is, if you still want the lunch I lovingly prepared for you three hours ago. I've had *mine*. Got tired of waiting.'

Inside, Mo's house was dark and musty, the awnings drawn down to shut out the glaring summer sun. Eloise sidled along the narrow hallway after Dad, trying not to knock anything over. Books tottered in piles on the floor, spilled from shelves, slid from heaps on chairs and tables.

'What's for lunch? Hope we haven't come all this way for one of your famous baked-bean jaffles!' called Dad. He winked at Eloise. 'Don't be scared of Mo,' he whispered. 'She loves a good fight. You have to stand up to her.'

Dad and Eloise squeezed themselves into chairs and Mo banged bowls onto the dining table. 'It's soup.'

Eloise spooned it up and let it trickle back into the bowl. Unidentifiable lumps floated in a steaming pinkish-brown liquid.

'Got the recipe from the next-door neighbours,' said Mo. 'Beetroots were on special this week, apparently. I was just making up another batch.'

'Thought beetroots were a winter thing.' Dad slurped warily. 'Mm. That's not bad, actually.' He flashed Mo his most charming grin.

Eloise lifted her spoon cautiously to her lips. There was a flavour she couldn't quite identify. Mo was watching her across the table. Eloise's heart began to thump again. She chased a thread of yoghurt with her spoon and it dissolved into nothing.

'Magnificent. I'm impressed.' Dad laid down his spoon and cleared his throat. 'Actually, Mo, there was a small favour I wanted to ask.'

Mo folded her arms. 'Spit it out.'

'Accommodation,' said Dad. 'For Eloise. Just for a few weeks, while I'm running around. I've got to go back to the city for a while, finalise the investors, talk to architects, put the plans together, that kind of thing.'

'Why couldn't she stay where she was?'

'That was . . . only temporary. Not suitable.' Dad didn't say anything about Bree.

Eloise had never liked Bree much. Bree always called her Ellie. Bree thought Eloise was weird.

'She can't stay here,' said Mo flatly. 'There's nowhere to put her.'

'What about my old room?'

'Excuse me; you haven't lived here for seventeen years. Things change. That's my study now.'

'You're not still writing that book, are you? The same one? The boat thing?'

'*A Brief History of Sea Voyages*, yes.'

'Brief? You've only been writing it for twenty years! Lucky it's not a *long* history!'

'Hilarious,' said Mo coldly.

'Not to mention the fact that you've never even *seen* the sea—'

'Haven't you heard of the internet, Stephen?'

They glared at each other. Then Dad said, more cajolingly, 'How about that old flop-out in the sunroom, is that still there? She won't mind roughing it for a while, she's used to it. Aren't you, Elder Statesman? As long as she's got her pencils and paper, she's happy.'

Eloise stared at the tablecloth. Her stomach was turning corkscrews.

'She doesn't look happy to me,' said Mo. 'Maybe you should have discussed this plan with her before. Maybe you should have discussed it with *me*.'

'She's your granddaughter; you haven't seen her since she was four. I thought you'd love to spend some time with her!'

'No, you didn't. You only thought about what was convenient for *you*.'

'Come on, Mo. It's not like you've got anything better to do—'

'Just the small matter of my *work*.'

'Oh please. You call that work?'

'You think you've done better, do you? Dragging that poor kid around since Anna died. What kind of life is that for a child? Look at her! She hasn't spoken a word since she arrived! What's wrong with her?'

There was a terrible silence.

'There's nothing wrong with Eloise,' said Dad.

'When did she stop speaking? Or didn't you notice?'

'She's just quiet. She lives in her own world. She always has, even when Anna was—'

There was a rapping at the back door. Dad folded his arms, and for a moment he and Mo glared at each other, chins jutting, like mirror images. Then Mo said grimly, 'I am not going to take responsibility for your damaged child. That's your job, not mine. Is that clear?'

She pushed back her chair and marched out of the room.

Dad glanced at Eloise. 'All right, Electron Microscope?'

A tear ran down the side of Eloise's nose. She shook her head.

'Oh Lord,' muttered Dad. 'Not *now* . . .'

There were voices in the hall. Then Mo reappeared in the doorway, propelling before her a dark-haired boy a year or two older than Eloise. He held a cardboard box full of groceries.

'Tommy Durrani,' announced Mo. 'From next door. He does all my errands. Worth his weight in gold, this boy. Be lost without him.'

Tommy mumbled something and ducked his head. His grey eyes were fringed with long lashes.

Dad jumped up and thrust out his hand. 'Pleasure to meet you, young man. Tommy, was it? Glad to hear you're taking such good care of my old mum.'

Tommy shook the tips of Dad's fingers, hampered by the box in his arms.

'My son, Stephen. My granddaughter, Eloise,' said Mo.

Tommy looked at Eloise. 'You coming to stay?'

Eloise stared at her soup bowl. Another tear stung at her eye but didn't fall.

'Eloise *might* be staying here for a little while,' Mo said grudgingly at last.

'Wonderful!' Dad shouted. 'That's marvellous. Thanks, Mo. Thanks, err . . . Tommy.' He fumbled for his wallet and tried to press a fifty-dollar note into Tommy's hand. But Tommy stepped sharply backward.

'I don't help Mrs Mo for money.' He scowled, and turned to Mo. 'I'll put this in the kitchen.' He vanished, and a minute later they heard the back door click shut.

Pink-faced, Dad shoved the fifty dollars back into his wallet.

'Not everybody lives for the almighty dollar, believe it or not,' said Mo. 'A thoroughly nice boy, that Tommy. His family's been in Turner nearly two years now. Sydney before that. The mother's our local doctor. The father used to be a professor in Afghanistan. Hasn't got a job here yet.'

'Professor of what?' Dad was grumpy now.

'Psychology.'

'Huh,' said Dad.

'Don't say it,' warned Mo.

Dad spread his hands. 'Say what?'

Eloise didn't know what either, but then Mo spun around and fixed her with a ferocious stare. 'As for you, young lady, you need a rest. Think I can't recognise an over-tired child when I see one? Go and lie down on my bed.'

Eloise froze, but Dad nudged her. 'Go on. Mo's right. We've had a long day, and a late one last night.'

Mo swept Eloise into her bedroom. Numbly, Eloise removed her shoes and scrambled onto the high white bed. Mo grunted and closed the door.

Eloise lay flat on her back and gazed up at the blotchy ceiling. It was a relief to be alone. People tired her out, especially new people. A murmur of voices came from the living room. Probably Dad and Mo were talking about her. She rolled onto her side and pulled a pillow over her ear.

Even with the awning down, Mo's bedroom was like an oven; the sun had baked the roof all afternoon. The world was getting hotter and hotter, Eloise knew that. But there were lots of things she didn't know. Bree had told Dad she was *unbelievably naïve*. That was one of the things Eloise wasn't supposed to hear. But she was pretty sure that Bree had never seen a ghost . . .

A shiver ran across Eloise's skin. She sat up and looked around for a pen or a piece of paper, but there was nothing to draw with. She lay back down and imagined the ceiling was a sheet of paper. She raised one hand and traced the shape of the girl in the air: the grey shadows behind her, the pale outline of her dress, the dark cloud of the girl's hair beneath her hat. Eloise moved her hand this way and that, tilting the invisible pencil, slowly filling in the blankness with lines, with smudges and shadings of grey. A mist of sadness spread through her as she realised something she hadn't really noticed at the time: the ghostly girl was so *happy*. Eloise hadn't been happy like that since . . . not for a long time . . .

Curled on the white bedspread, Eloise fell asleep.

3

It was cold. Eloise pressed herself into the mattress. Her head swirled with images of floating pale figures, sunken ships, dark ribbons of seaweed twined through portholes. She was swimming from room to room, swimming after a ghostly girl who drifted just ahead of her. A voice called, *I'm coming!* But Eloise didn't know if it was herself who spoke, or the girl she was chasing through the dim green water. Eloise swam through the dark, deeper and deeper, colder and colder, until she shivered awake.

The first three seconds after Eloise woke were always the same. In the first second, she knew there was something she had to remember, but she didn't know what it was.

In the next second she did remember. *Mum*.

In the third second she squashed that knowledge into the tightest ball she could and wedged it right into the very back of her mind, so she could pretend it wasn't there. Then she opened her eyes.

Eloise blinked. All the things that didn't really matter came flooding in: Dad, the house, Mo, the boy next door.

The bedroom was almost dark. Eloise slid unsteadily off the bed and stumbled out into the hall. Mo was in the kitchen, dipping a chunk of bread into a bowl of beetroot soup. She gestured to the stove. 'Plenty left if you want some. Bread's on the bench.'

Eloise looked around for Dad.

'He's gone,' said Mo. 'Back to the city. Sent you his love. Said he'll be back soon.'

A lump came into Eloise's throat. Mo grimaced. 'Couldn't face saying goodbye to you, so he ran away. We McCredies are good at running from our problems. Runs in the family, you could say. Ha!' She scooped up a spoonful of soup. 'Go on, sit down. Don't stand there like a shag on a rock. Eat something.'

They sat on either side of the kitchen table in

silence. Presently Mo pushed her bowl aside and looked at Eloise over the top of her glasses. 'Since we seem to be stuck with each other for the time being, we'd better set up some rules of the house.' She ticked them off on her fingers. 'One: you don't disturb me while I'm working. Two: my study is out of bounds. At *all* times. Is that clear?'

Eloise nodded.

'Three . . .' Mo stopped, and sighed. 'How shall I put this? You might think I'm a crazy old woman, but the fact is, I don't . . . I don't like to leave the house any more.' She narrowed her eyes at Eloise. 'Young Tommy runs my errands and so forth these days, bless him, and his mother's been kind enough to pop in and have a look at me if I'm ever sick, which, touch wood,' she rapped on the table, making Eloise jump, 'so far, I haven't been, very. The point is, I'm not going to *ferry you about*. Understand? You want to do any,' she waved her hand vaguely, '*activities* – netball or soccer or hanging about the train station or whatever it is the young do for fun these days – you organise it yourself. There's a bicycle in the garage and a helmet somewhere, you're welcome to use them. Just don't get into trouble . . . Ha! That can be rule number three: don't get into any trouble. That should cover most eventualities.' Mo popped a piece of bread into her mouth. 'You could get Tommy to show you around. He knows what's what.'

Eloise kept her face neutral. She didn't want to join in any kind of activities; *activities* filled her with dread. At the last few schools she'd been to, she'd spent most of her time avoiding them. And she certainly wasn't going to trail around after that boy; she'd die of embarrassment. At least Mo wasn't going to make her do anything.

'And, of course, there are rules about water,' Mo was saying. 'Dishes are washed in that little tub in the sink. Three and a half minutes for showers; there's a timer in the bathroom. Make sure you put the plug in, I bucket the grey water onto the garden. And the toilet. You know the old rhyme?'

Eloise looked at her blankly.

'If it's yellow, let it mellow. If it's brown, flush it down. Understand? Good.' Mo pressed her lips together and rose to her feet. 'I think we'll manage quite well, after all. Now I'm going to do some work. You want to watch television? It's in the living room.'

Eloise shook her head, and Mo shrugged. 'Suit yourself. I've made up your bed in the sunroom. Your bags are in there.' She shuffled away to her study and soon Eloise heard the faint clackety-clack of a computer keyboard. She took a chunk of bread and went to find the sunroom.

It was hardly even a room, just a tiny alcove beside the back door. The laundry, the back toilet and the back door all opened off it. The fold-out sofa filled almost the whole space; it had been made up into a bed, the sheets tucked in savagely tight. There was no table, not even a shelf, nowhere for Eloise to unpack.

But she didn't mind that. Bree had a very neat apartment, all shiny and bare, and she made such a fuss if she found any of Eloise's things 'cluttering up the place' that Eloise had ended up living out of her bags and never unpacking anything. The single bed in Bree's junk room had become Eloise's private island, her lifeboat in someone else's ocean. Mo's fold-out was a double bed. Eloise stretched in luxury.

She wondered when Dad would come back. He'd said soon – maybe tomorrow. He was always coming and going these days; she didn't like it, but she was used to it. And Mo was going to leave her alone. If it was only a day, or a couple of days, she'd be all right. Though Mo had been talking as if it would be longer than that.

Her stomach was starting to tie itself in knots, so she sat cross-legged on the bed and pulled out her sketchpad and pencils. She flipped to a blank page and started to scribble. The knots in her stomach loosened when she drew. First she sketched the big white house, almost drowned between the trees. Then she drew the pattern in the glass panels by the front door. As she shaded the triangles, swinging the page this way and that, her heart calmed.

She took a fresh page and drew Mo as she'd first seen her, brandishing a knife, her hair writhing like snakes. Drawing the witchiness made Eloise see that Mo really wasn't as scary as she'd thought. She looked at that picture for a while, pleased with it.

Next she drew the boy who'd brought Mo's shopping. Eloise wasn't good with names. But his face came alive under her pencil: strong nose, straight-across eyebrows, long eyelashes, curling hair, a soft mouth. He frowned out of the page at her, as if he were annoyed about being captured in her book.

Now she was ready. Now she'd draw the girl on
the stairs: the big hat, the tripping feet, the fingers
light on the rail. But her pencil stuck; she couldn't
transfer her memory onto the paper. She traced a
tentative line; stopped; drew another. Her heart was
beating fast again. It was all wrong—

'*Eloise!*'

She jumped, and slammed her book shut. Mo
glared from the doorway. 'What are you, deaf? Didn't
you hear me? It's almost midnight.'

Eloise blinked, startled.

'Not that I care, particularly, but apparently it's good
for young people to go to bed at a reasonable hour.
When I was your age, I used to stay up all night reading
with a torch under the blankets. Ruined my eyes. So
if you must stay up reading or scribbling or whatever,
please keep the light on. What's that, your sketchpad?
No, it's all right; you don't have to show me. One thing
I can do is mind my own business. Good night.'

Mo stalked away, and when she'd gone, Eloise
leaned from the raft of the bed and clicked off the
light. She lay awake for a long time, staring into
the dark, trying to think about nothing, before sleep
pulled her under at last.

Eloise's eyes flew open. Something was rattling near her head. Then a voice called, 'Hello, Mrs Mo?'

Eloise sat straight up in bed and found herself staring into the startled grey eyes of the boy from next door. He had pushed the door open as he called out to Mo and had almost tripped over the end of Eloise's bed. And there she was in just her singlet.

The boy's face flushed deep red. 'Sorry . . . didn't . . .' he mumbled and backed away, almost falling down the steps. The screen door banged and sprang open again behind him.

Eloise hurled herself out of bed, pulled on her T-shirt and shorts and slid her feet into her thongs. She heard the front doorbell chime, then Mo's slippers shuffled down the hallway and there were voices at the front door.

'Tommy? You're very formal today.'

Then, very muffled, '. . . back door . . . the girl . . .'

Mo, loud and brisk, 'Gave you a fright, did she? Don't pull that face. Come and have a proper look at her; you'll see she's nothing to be scared of.'

Eloise didn't wait to hear more; she flew out the

back door. The garage had old-fashioned double doors that gaped apart. She squeezed through the crack, heart racing.

'Eloise?' Mo banged the back door open and called into the yard. 'Elo-*ise!*' There was a pause, then the screen door slammed again as Mo went back inside.

Now was her chance. There was the bicycle – a faded-red boy's bike, propped against the garage wall. Eloise dragged it outside, swung up into the saddle and wobbled down the driveway. The bike was too big for her, and the tyres were soft; she had to push hard. She jammed her feet down on the pedals and flew out into the street, the hot wind in her hair.

She zoomed round one corner, then another. She'd never ridden so fast without a helmet before. She felt wild and reckless. Her shadow dipped and swayed on the broad black ribbon of the road.

The big red-brick church crouched at the top of the hill, and Eloise pedalled toward it. She knew where to go. The last time she'd ridden a bike was when she and Dad had first moved in with Bree, when Bree was still pretending they could be a family. One weekend they'd all ridden along the river.

She remembered calling to Dad to slow down, so it must have been before she went quiet.

That was how she thought of it, *going quiet*. It had happened gradually. Somehow there was less and less to say, and now she seemed to have forgotten how to speak at all. Bree and Dad pretended not to notice; maybe they'd got used to it, too. It was a bit of a shock when Mo had pointed out that it wasn't normal.

Maybe Mo would get used to it, too.

The wheels hissed softly on the pine needle carpet as Eloise pushed the bike down the driveway. Glowing with sweat, she dropped the bike near the front door.

The long grass at the back of the house must have been a lawn once, but now it was so high that the crisp blades brushed Eloise's fingertips. Maybe there were snakes. The grass shifted and swayed in the hot, dry wind. Eloise looked up at the silent house with its blank, blind windows, but no ghostly face peered out at her.

At the bottom of the slope she spied the shabby roof of a small pavilion, and the scaffolding of a diving board. A swimming pool! Eloise swished eagerly through the grass.

The pool was screened from the house by a grove of trees and bushes. The pool was empty, of course, and littered with dead leaves. It wasn't long, but it was deep, lined with tiny blue and green tiles, with bald patches where the tiles had flaked away.

Beside the pool stood a hexagonal summerhouse with an arched doorway, its pillars wound around and overgrown with ivy. Eloise pushed aside a curtain of vines and stepped inside.

Once, it had been painted white, but the paint had peeled from the walls. Inside the summerhouse was quiet and still, as if she'd stepped into another world. Eloise was enchanted. She ducked outside again, eyes screwed shut against the sun, and the noise of cicadas burst over her. They shrilled louder and louder, blotting out all other sounds, and then, abruptly, switched off. Eloise opened her eyes and blinked.

The garden was transformed.

The long dry grass had contracted to a shaggy green lawn, the tangled trees had shrunk and neatened, banks of flowering bushes had exploded into existence. A neat white fence ran between the pool and the screening trees. And beyond the trees, the house was bright and white and fresh. It sat up straight and alert, not sad and tilted any more.

Eloise's stomach jolted, like being in a plane when the ground drops away below. For a minute she was paralysed, frozen where she stood.

Then slowly she turned her head and saw that the pool was filled with blue shimmering water.

Eloise caught her breath. Could it be real? She knelt and dabbled her fingers in the water. It was clean and clear . . . She hesitated for a second, then stripped off to her underwear and slipped into the pool. The cold made her gasp. She shook her hair back and dived down as deep as she could, a needle through cool silk. The green and blue tiles shimmered and glowed; the pool was filled with light. Eloise brushed the bottom of the pool with her fingertips, the smooth lustrous tiles like the inside of a seashell, and kicked herself back up to the surface. Her head broke through and she pushed the wet hair from her eyes.

Someone clapped their hands.

Eloise's heart jumped into her throat and she

twisted around. A girl sat on the edge of the pool, dangling bare legs into the water. A broad-brimmed hat was pushed to the back of her head.

'Hello,' said the girl. 'Where did you come from?'

4

Eloise said nothing. In confusion, she dived again, right to the bottom, half-hoping that the girl would be gone when she came up again.

But she wasn't; she was still sitting there, watching. Although it seemed she didn't expect an answer to her question. Instead she crunched into an apple, and held another out to Eloise. 'Want one?'

Eloise swam over to the side of the pool and heaved herself out, dripping. Suddenly she was conscious of having wet underwear and no towel. The girl must have understood because she scrambled up, darted into the summerhouse and emerged with a slightly dusty dark-blue towel, which Eloise hastily wrapped around herself.

'There are spare towels, and hats, and *paranephalia* like that in there,' said the girl, sitting down again. 'But I've told them, it's *my* place. I don't want their stuff all over it. It's not fair.'

Eloise wondered if she'd stepped into a dream. Everything was different. The air was cooler. There were clouds in the sky where none had been before. The garden was so *neat*. And the summerhouse looked different too. The ivy that had almost hidden it had shrunk back to reveal sturdy arches, and the curtain of vines that had hung over the doorway was gone.

The other girl bit into her apple. 'The summerhouse is just for me. Mumma and Dad said so. Come and see!' She jumped up, and Eloise followed.

The inside was transformed. A swathe of spangled blue cloth wound around the central pillar; odd patches of carpet were scattered on the floor. Someone had begun to daub fresh white paint on one wall and then got bored, or run out of paint. All the dead leaves had been swept away, and light poured in through the arched doorway.

'Isn't it *splendufferous*?' The girl hugged herself in satisfaction. She was younger than Eloise had thought at first, younger than Eloise herself, though anyone who saw them together would probably think they were the same age. Her straight, dark, silky hair was tied back in a ponytail. She had fierce green eyes, and a small pointed chin. She was wearing a kind of pinafore dress, and her feet were bare. 'My place,' she repeated firmly, as if Eloise had contradicted her. 'But I'll share it with you if you like.'

Eloise made a small movement with her head, meaning that she didn't mind, the other girl didn't have to share if she didn't want to, but the girl seemed to take this as agreement, because she gave Eloise a sudden radiant smile.

'Oh, good!' she cried. 'You can help me fix it up. Dad said he'd help me paint it but he's too busy.' She jerked her chin up the slope. 'Busy with the big house.' She pulled a face.

Eloise thought of her own dad, and how, very soon, he would be busy with *their* house— But of course it was the same house . . . Wasn't it? So that meant this was her summerhouse, too . . .

The other girl seized Eloise's arm. 'There's lots of stuff lying round, from the builders, wood and paint and everything. Do you like painting?'

Eloise half-shrugged, half-nodded.

'Good, 'cause I don't. You can be in charge of painting. Come on, let's get some.'

Eloise grabbed her clothes and pulled them on, then the summerhouse girl dragged her through the garden, along twisting little hidden paths between bushes laden with purple flowers and starred with white blossom.

'Come this way,' she hissed in Eloise's ear, so close it tickled. 'So no one'll see us. There're always too many people.' She pulled the same disdainful face as before. Suddenly her grip tightened on Eloise's arm. 'Ssh! Listen. Hear that?'

The summerhouse girl and Eloise froze in the bushes, not far from the house. Above their heads, from an open window, music floated down: the same broken phrase of cello, over and over. Someone swore, and the music stopped abruptly. The summerhouse girl clapped her hand over her mouth to stop a giggle escaping, and Eloise smiled. A laugh was bubbling up inside Eloise, fizzing like lemonade. The feeling surprised her; she realised she hadn't laughed for a long time. Not since she *went quiet* – maybe not since Mum . . . Mum was always laughing, always singing to herself. She'd sing silly words to make Eloise laugh too, and then she'd scoop her up and spin her round till they were both breathless with laughing . . .

Eloise smacked that thought down hard.

The summerhouse girl tugged her onward, squeezing between the bushes – deadly serious again, as if they were spies and their lives were at stake.

They emerged from the garden on the far side of the house, the side Eloise hadn't seen, near a cluster of sheds and garages and outbuildings. The summerhouse girl darted from one building to the next, beckoning Eloise to follow. Once, they heard voices, a slammed door, and had to freeze, pressing themselves desperately against the wall. The girl's green eyes were wide with almost-real terror, and Eloise remembered something else from long ago that she'd nearly forgotten. She remembered what it was like to *play*, to believe in your own game so hard it choked you.

The summerhouse girl grabbed her hand again, and together they darted into a shed fragrant with sawdust and crammed with carpenters' rubbish, chunks of wood, curled shavings, plans and pencils. The summerhouse girl picked up a big tin dribbled

all over with white paint. Eloise could see from the
way she carried it that it was almost empty. 'I've got
brushes,' the girl whispered. 'Come on, let's go.'

They crashed back through the bushes, faster
and more careless than before, and by the time they
reached the safety of the summerhouse, the other
girl was giggling out loud. She dropped her tin on
the bench and collapsed with a gurgle of laughter.
Eloise sat down, feeling much older and more sober.
Her undies were still damp and uncomfortable, and
whose paint had they taken? What if someone came
looking for it?

After a minute or two the summerhouse girl sat
up, wiped her eyes, and tugged up a section of bench
to reveal a storage place. She rummaged around
and pulled out two big shaggy paintbrushes. Then
she took a spoon and tried to pry off the paint lid,
without success.

'Are you going to help or not?' she said, after some
struggle, and frowned up at Eloise. She poked a long
strand of hair behind her ear, where it immediately
fell forward again.

Eloise looked at her. She knew her own face was
creased up with anxiety, a hard lump in her throat.

43

Suddenly she felt dizzy, the ground spinning down and away. Where was this place? Who was this girl? What was she doing here?

Eloise jumped up and ran out of the summerhouse into the blinding sunlight. There was an instant of silence while the world slid out of focus before Eloise's eyes, and then the cicadas roared.

Everything was back to the way it had been before. The pool was empty, the garden tangled, the grass high and yellow. The white fence had disappeared. Eloise turned and pushed back into the summerhouse, but the girl was gone, everything was gone. It was empty. Without looking, she knew that the house had gone dead too, blind and abandoned, slumped into the hill again.

Eloise pressed her hands to her forehead, trying to understand. She'd seen a movie once about an enchanted garden. But that was just a story; things like this didn't happen in her world.

The sun had slid mysteriously down the sky. Eloise was ravenous and ragingly thirsty. What had happened? The garden was neglected, unkempt, unhealthy. And it was boiling hot again. She wasn't imagining that. The cicadas shrieked in a steady din that filled her ears and wouldn't let her think.

A trickle of sweat ran down Eloise's neck. She began to run. The long grass clutched her ankles. If the bike was gone . . .

But the old bicycle was exactly where she'd left it, tipped over on the weed-strewn gravel. Eloise bent over and gasped for breath. Of course the bike was there. Where else would it be? She was fine. She was safe.

But *something* had happened. And something had happened in the house yesterday, too. She'd seen two girls now. Or maybe it was the same girl . . . They could have been the same girl . . . But the summerhouse girl was no ghost. She'd grabbed Eloise's hand; her breath had tickled her ear; she was real. So who was she? Where could she have come from?

Trembling, Eloise climbed onto the saddle of the bike and pushed off with one foot, faster and faster, back down the shadowed tunnel of pines toward the outside world.

5

Mo lowered her glasses to the tip of her nose and glared at Eloise. 'I don't care what you get up to. I don't care where you go. That's not the point. I'm sure you can look after yourself, and the streets are safer than they ever were. But running off the way you did this morning was downright rude, and it will *not* happen again.'

Eloise hung her head. She'd forgotten that she'd run away to avoid that Tommy boy.

'He came over to invite us to dinner – don't panic, I said no. Not for your benefit, I might add. I'd rather cut my hand off than go to dinner in someone else's house. Don't tell anyone I said that.' Mo looked at her. 'No, I don't suppose you will. Where were you today, anyway? You're covered in scratches. Did you go to the creek? Or the trickle, as we should call it these days, so they tell me.'

Eloise shook her head.

Mo stared at her hard. 'But you're all right. No traumatic experiences.'

Eloise wondered if seeing ghosts, if that was what she'd done, or going into another world, counted as traumatic experiences. She thought for a second, then shook her head again.

'Next time Tommy comes over I expect you to . . . well, shake his hand, at least.' Eloise nodded, and Mo sighed. 'You don't make things easy for yourself, do you? All right, buzz off and let me get back to my sea voyages.' She turned back to her computer and began to type.

Eloise eased the study door closed. She took a packet of biscuits from the kitchen cupboard and retreated to her fold-out bed, still unmade from the morning. Eloise took her sketchbook and pencils out from under her pillow and began to draw the summerhouse.

As the lines curled from the tip of her pencil,

Eloise's thoughts looped and snarled and slowly grew clearer. What had happened to her? She'd seen something. She'd *gone* somewhere. She must have gone back in time. She'd seen the house and the garden, the pool and the summerhouse as they used to be in the olden days, when they were new and lived in and cared for; when a family lived there, a little girl, someone who played the cello by an open window, a mother and a father who gave their daughter the summerhouse to play in.

Somehow time had jumped backward, and dragged her back with it like a wave sucking at a beach. Then it had rushed forward and dumped her back in her own time again. She had walked through some kind of invisible wall into the past.

Eloise flipped to a clear page and smoothed it with her hand. Then she began to draw the face of the summerhouse girl: her big fierce eyes, her pointed chin, the small beaked nose. When the drawing was almost done, Eloise faltered; she stared at the picture. Then she scrambled off the bed and up the hall to the bathroom. She craned to see her own face in the mirrored cabinet.

It was true: the summerhouse girl's face looked

like her own reflection. The same big eyes, the same beaky nose.

Mum used to call Eloise *my little owl*. And it was a little owl's face that Eloise had drawn in her sketchbook.

Eloise stood there for a long time, watching her own face in the mirror, as if the reflected girl might tell her something important. But she didn't say a word.

Next morning, before it got too hot, Eloise slipped from the house and pedalled the old bike toward the church on the hill. Today she was prepared. She'd found the helmet in the garage, and a pump to harden the tyres. She wore bathers under her dress. A dress was more old-fashioned than shorts, more suitable. As well as her sketchpad and pencils, she'd packed apples and biscuits and a bottle of water. Luckily Mo seemed to live mostly on biscuits; the cupboard was full of them.

She'd run into Mo in the kitchen and half-expected to be questioned about where she was going, but Mo had just looked her up and down, observing Eloise's hat, the water bottle, the backpack. 'Good girl,' she said. 'You look ready for anything.' Then she'd shuffled off to her study and closed the door.

The house lay becalmed among the trees, mute and still. Eloise propped her bicycle (already she thought of it as her own) in the shade by the front steps and stood for a moment, listening. Her pulse raced.

She couldn't expect it to happen every time. She wasn't sure if she wanted it to happen or not. And what was 'it' anyway? Time travel, magic, ghosts?

Eloise walked slowly through the long grass. When she caught sight of the diving board, she closed her eyes and pictured the house as she'd seen it yesterday. She took one tentative step forward, then another. The dry grass crunched under her runners, and the sun was hot on the back of her neck.

If she really wanted it, so badly it hurt in her chest, it wouldn't happen. Things you wanted as badly as that never did. She had to pretend she didn't care; she had to trick it into happening.

One cicada began to shrill, then another and another. Eloise halted, her eyes still squeezed shut. It wasn't going to work. She'd hoped too hard . . .

Then the cicadas stopped.

Every sound switched off. Eloise's eyes flew open.

The garden was crowded with green and splashed with flowers, the lawn cropped roughly underfoot, the pool brimming with liquid light. Music floated down the slope from the house; this time someone was playing a piano.

And the girl was leaning out of the summerhouse, beckoning frantically to Eloise. 'Quick, quick, they'll *see* you!'

Eloise ran, and the summerhouse girl pulled her inside. 'They mustn't see you,' she said earnestly. 'You're my *comfidential* friend.' Eloise must have looked blank, because the girl added impatiently, 'My *secret* friend. No one's allowed to see you but me.'

Eloise froze. She stepped back, so the girl's hand fell from her arm. What would happen if she became trapped here, in the wrong time, if she could never get back? No one would ever know what had happened to her. No one could ever find her. What had seemed mysterious and exciting suddenly felt dangerous, threatening.

Eloise flew to the doorway and hovered there like a trapped bird, staring out. What if she ran out of the garden? Where could she go? The house was full of people. Where was Dad? Probably he wasn't born yet. Perhaps even Mo wasn't born yet. And if Eloise couldn't find her way out, she would never be born either. But if she was never born, she couldn't be here in the first place, so . . . would she just snuff out, like a candle?

Her head whirled; she felt giddy. She sank onto the bench and leaned her head against the wall.

The summerhouse girl watched her. 'Are you all right? You look sick. Do you want a drink of water?'

Eloise had forgotten about her backpack. She tugged out her water bottle and gulped thankfully.

'Don't be sick,' said the girl. ''Cause look . . . I got some more paint. You're in charge of the painting, remember? Why didn't you come yesterday? I cleaned the walls all by myself with a bucket, look.' She pointed reproachfully to the walls, which were, indeed, much cleaner.

So a whole day had passed for the summerhouse girl, but not for Eloise. Time clearly ran differently, at different speeds, in the two places – or should that be the two *times*, because the *place* was the same . . . Eloise's head began to whirl again, and to stop it she jumped up and seized the tin of white paint and a wide brush. The summerhouse girl clapped her hands in delight.

'It's going to look *splendufferous*! Let's do the inside first and then the outside. Only I wish we could paint it all different colours, pink and blue and yellow, but Dad said I could only use white. I said could I put *Anna's House* over the door, so people *know* it's my place, but he said no to that too—'

Anna.

Eloise's hand shook so violently that the paintbrush fell to the floor.

'Ooh, careful! Lucky you didn't put any paint on yet,' cried the summerhouse girl. Eloise bent down and picked up the brush with trembling fingers.

The girl's name was Anna. Eloise's mum was called Anna.

Eloise forced the paint tin open and dipped in the brush. She swished a wide white streak over the planks, up and back, following the grain of the wood. Anna. *Anna.* She peeked over her shoulder at the other girl, at Anna, who was still chattering away as she swept dust out through the doorway, something about her dad, and how her mother had gone away for the summer.

Eloise looked like her mother, everyone said so, except for her hair. Her name was Anna.

The white paint slapped back and forth across the wall. Eloise hardly saw it. This was her mother, her mother as a little girl. She was alive: a live, talking, giggling little girl, warm and breathing, darting around. And she wanted to be Eloise's friend, and Eloise had pushed her away . . .

Eloise let the brush fall again. She rushed to Anna and grabbed her hand.

Anna looked up, laughing. 'What's the matter?'

Eloise, confused, let her hand drop. She didn't know what to do. She couldn't hug this strange girl or kiss her. This little girl wasn't her lost mum. Not the mum who'd sung and swirled red and gold in the kitchen, not the mum who'd cradled her in her warm lap and whispered in her hair. But . . . she was. She just didn't know it.

Eloise felt her face go pink. She shook her head and flipped her hands in the air to say sorry, and then she felt tears rise in her eyes.

'Do you feel sick again?' Anna said. 'Is it the

paint smell making you *nautilus*? Sometimes it makes my mumma feel sick. How can you be an artist if paint makes you sick, I'd like to know. Maybe you should have another drink of water. Are you going to throw up?'

Eloise shook her head and stumbled out of the summerhouse. The sun from the pool dazzled her eyes, searing bright. Tears spilled down her cheeks and she scrubbed them away.

She heard Anna's voice behind her, an anguished wail. 'Don't go away! You can't go yet!'

But then Anna's voice and all the other noises faded into the familiar well of silence, and Eloise's eyes opened onto the empty pool, the neglected garden. And when the shrill of the cicadas burst over her, it sounded like jeering.

6

The day after that was a scorcher, baking hot and windy. Mo's radio in the kitchen muttered about *fire danger* and *total fire ban*, and when Eloise opened the back door, the hot wind buffeted her face like a dragon's breath.

'You're not riding a bike around in this,' said Mo firmly. 'You'll get heatstroke.'

Reluctantly Eloise shut the door. Anna might be upset if she didn't come. But then, if the two times did run at different speeds, maybe Eloise could skip a day in her own time without missing one in Anna's . . . It was very confusing.

Also, she'd left her backpack and her hat behind in Anna's time. She'd taken them off in the summerhouse and when the time-wave caught her, she'd been dumped back in her own time without them.

The worst thing was that her sketchbook was in the backpack; being without that was like missing her hand. If she went back to the summerhouse now, in her own time, would she find the hat and the backpack still there, decayed and rotting and coated with cobwebs? But Anna would have moved them, wouldn't she? Would she – Eloise went cold all over – would she look at Eloise's drawings? Would it matter? What would she see? Her own house falling down. Her own garden overgrown with weeds. The faces of strangers. Were there secrets from the future that Eloise had drawn, things that a child from the past shouldn't see? Well, there was nothing she could do about it.

Mo was shut inside her study, writing about sea voyages. Her typing sounded like the pecking of angry birds. Eloise drifted from room to stuffy room. She slouched in front of the TV for a while, but Mo only had three channels and one of them was cricket. It made her think of Dad; he was always too impatient for cricket. Eloise clicked the TV off. She wondered when Dad was coming back.

Books tottered in towers in every corner and spilled from shelves against every wall. But reading was hard work for Eloise. Words were slippery to handle, and she often lost interest in a story before she could struggle to the end. Mum used to help her, but now Eloise had fallen behind at school. She loved to look at pictures, but Mo didn't seem to have any books with pictures in them.

When the phone rang, Eloise jumped. The telephone was in the kitchen, an old-fashioned handset hung on the wall. Eloise realised she'd never heard it ring before.

Of course she couldn't answer it. She stood in the hallway while the bell shrilled. Mo came out of the study and stood there too, with her hand on the wall. She didn't move to pick it up; she seemed to be waiting for it to stop. But it didn't stop; it went on and on ringing. Eloise realised that Mo didn't have an answering machine to cut in and make it stop.

At last Mo swore under her breath, strode past Eloise and snatched the phone off the wall.

'Yes?' Mo glanced at Eloise. 'It's your father,' she said.

Eloise took the handpiece and pressed it to her ear.

'Hello, El for Liquorice!' Dad sounded even heartier than usual. 'How's tricks? Keeping out of trouble? Things are going well here, *really* well. Got some really promising investors lined up, well . . . *potential* investors. One who's *genuinely* interested; we've had several meetings . . . Shouldn't be away too much longer. I'll be back before Christmas, *definitely*.'

Eloise had forgotten about Christmas. How far away was that?

'Fingers crossed, eh,' Dad was saying. 'Just wanted to say hi, touch base, you know. Is your grandmother there?'

Eloise held the phone out to Mo, who took it gingerly, as though it might bite, and listened for a minute.

'No, she's all right.' She looked at Eloise as she spoke. 'Keeping herself amused . . . No, she hasn't. Not to me, anyway . . . I hardly think that's my responsibility, Stephen . . . If you couldn't succeed, I hardly think I will . . . No, I will not go cap in hand to the neighbours, begging for psychiatric services . . . For pity's sake, isn't it obvious? Makes no difference to me. All right, goodbye.'

Mo crashed the phone back on its holder and scowled. 'Sends his love,' she said, and stomped off back to the study.

Every evening, Mo emptied the buckets of grey washing water onto her garden. That night, for the first time, Eloise helped too. She staggered with the sloshing bucket into the backyard and tipped it where Mo pointed. A beautiful smell rose up from the wet earth: a fresh, clean, clear smell. Eloise closed her eyes and breathed it in.

'Good evening, Mrs Mo,' came a polite voice from behind them. 'Good evening, Eloise.'

Eloise spun round and saw the head of Tommy from next door pop up over the fence that divided their backyards. He rested his arms on the fence and gazed down at them.

Mo put her hand on her chest. 'Haven't you ever heard of knocking?' she growled. 'Nearly gave me a flaming heart attack.'

Tommy grinned, and his rather solemn face lit up. 'I'm sorry. I heard your buckets; I knew you must be in the garden.'

'Still could have knocked,' said Mo severely.

'What do you want?'

'My parents would like to invite you and Eloise—'

'To dinner?' finished Mo. She lowered her bucket and wiped her hands on her trousers. Suddenly she looked very tired. 'That's kind of them. It's not that I don't appreciate it. But I'm afraid I can't accept.'

'Okay,' said Tommy amiably, and his head vanished as abruptly as it had appeared.

Mo wrapped her arms around herself, though it was still very warm outside. 'Come on, Eloise,' she said crossly. 'Come inside.' And she scuttled back into the house, hunched over like a beetle.

They'd no sooner stacked the buckets in the laundry than the doorbell rang. Mo swore loudly. 'Now what?' She peered out through the spyhole.

'Peculiar,' she said. 'Nobody there.' She opened the door a crack and there on the mat at her feet lay a foil-covered casserole dish. Mo took a deep breath. 'Interfering bossy know-it-all neighbours,' she said, but her voice was mild. She lifted the foil and sniffed. 'Smells all right. Suppose we'd better not waste it, eh, Eloise?'

It was curry, and it tasted delicious.

The next morning Eloise was eating breakfast when the front doorbell rang again. She nearly choked on her cornflakes, but she didn't have time to run away before Mo led Tommy into the kitchen.

'Hold on, I'll make a list,' she was saying. 'And here's your dish. Compliments to the chef. Your father, was it, this time?'

Tommy smiled. 'How did you know?'

'Heavy hand with the cardamon, your father.'

'Mum's so busy at the hospital, or at the surgery,' said Tommy. 'Dad's had to learn to cook a lot of things.'

Mo clucked. 'Make sure your mother gets enough rest, won't you. We can't afford to lose her . . . Bread, eggs, sugar, apples. Might get some bacon this time. Like bacon, Eloise?'

Eloise, who'd been trying to make herself invisible, gave a fractional nod.

'Bacon then. And more of those chocolate biscuits, we seem to be getting through those.' Mo rummaged in the cupboards and scribbled on her list while Tommy reminded her of things she might have forgotten: soap, tissues, detergent.

It dawned on Eloise that Tommy must do Mo's

shopping every week. Then it occurred to her that Mo hadn't gone out once since she'd arrived, days ago. She remembered Mo saying that first night that she didn't like to leave the house. So she really meant it. But Mo wasn't that old; she could walk all right; she wasn't sick. Why would she want to stay home all the time?

Eloise realised with a start that Tommy was looking at her. Not staring, just peeping sideways from under his long lashes. And she remembered something else that Mo had said.

She scraped back her chair and slipped across the kitchen, not looking at Tommy. She didn't want to, but Mo had said she must. She held out her hand.

Tommy gazed at her, puzzled. Then a light of laughter came into his eyes and he gripped her hand and squeezed it. 'Hello.'

Mo looked up from the depths of the fridge where she was examining limp vegetables. 'Hah!' she said. 'Well done, Eloise. Eloise is shy,' she told Tommy. 'She'll be starting at your school next year, I suppose.'

'Oh.' Tommy let go of Eloise's hand. He was blocking the door so she couldn't escape. She stood there awkwardly for a second, then, because she didn't know what else to do, she sat down again and poured out more cornflakes.

'That's the lot,' announced Mo finally, and slammed the fridge door. 'Hold on, I'll get you that card.' She marched out of the room.

'The card to get her money,' explained Tommy. 'For the shopping. It's easier for her that way.'

Eloise nodded.

'Mrs Mo's your grandmother, yeah?' Tommy moved closer and lowered his voice. 'You know, she doesn't go out? Never, since we came here. Only into the backyard. Panic attacks, she told my mum. Makes her heart go . . .' Tommy's hand fluttered like a fish. 'You know what I mean?'

Eloise didn't, really.

'It's good you've come. Family, to look after her, eh? You and your dad?'

Eloise looked down into her cornflake bowl. She felt uncomfortable and vaguely accused. But she was only a kid; it wasn't her job to look after Mo. She wanted to go; she wanted to find Anna and get her sketchbook back. It wasn't quite so hot today. She felt greedy to see Anna again, to look for

Mum in the summerhouse girl's face. She was glad when Tommy took the card and the list and left, and when she heard the study door click, shutting Mo in.

Now she was free, and she hurried out of the house so fast her feet hardly skimmed the ground.

7

E very day, if it wasn't too hot, Eloise went to
the big house. Every time, the ritual was the
same. She'd drop her bike by the front steps,
walk across the grass, and shut her eyes.

Sometimes it took three steps, sometimes it was ten,
before the noises of the present faded out. There was
a dizzying moment of silence, of nothingness, and
then the sounds of the other time faded in, as if the
volume had been turned up – birdsong, the rustle of
leaves, faint music from the house, laughter – and her
eyes flew open, always just too late to catch the instant
of changeover, the plunge into the other world.

Anna was always there. If she wasn't already
waiting at the summerhouse when Eloise arrived,

she'd soon come running, complaining that her father had made her finish her breakfast, or that one of the guests had kept her talking. She pulled a face when she talked about the guests. 'I like it best when it's just Mumma and Dad and me,' she said. 'But it never is. That's why I'm glad *you're* here.'

At first Eloise thought that Anna was talking about friends who'd come to stay, but there seemed to be an awful lot of 'guests', and Anna didn't always know their names. Then Eloise wondered if the house was a hotel in Anna's time, too. It was strange that Dad had never mentioned it.

Gradually Eloise pieced together that the house was not a hotel – not an ordinary hotel, anyway. Anna's parents ran it. But this summer, because Anna's mother was away, her father was running it all by himself and that was why he was especially busy – too busy to spend much time with Anna. It was what was called an 'artists' retreat', where writers and painters and sculptors and musicians could come to work in peace.

Eloise thought she understood how they felt. Being in Anna's time, at the summerhouse, gave her a feeling of peace too. Perhaps it was because she knew she was in the past: nothing bad could happen there, because it would have happened already, and it hadn't, so it couldn't. She was safe there. At the summerhouse, she and Anna were inside their own private world, where nothing could touch them.

Sometimes a tilt of Anna's head or a half-smile would pierce Eloise's memory like the swift jab of a needle and she would be positive that Anna was her mother. At these moments, Eloise would long to grab Anna and squeeze her, to hold on to her and keep her safe forever. But then Anna would stamp and grumble about something, or she'd say a word differently from how Eloise's mum used to say it, and Eloise was not so sure.

Anna gave Eloise back her sketchbook. Eloise took it with a quick skip of the heart, because she never showed her pictures to anyone. But all Anna said was, 'You're a pretty good drawer. You're not as good as my mumma, but you're pretty good.'

Eloise felt her face grow hot as she shoved the book into her backpack. But after that she didn't mind if Anna saw her sketching. They'd often sit together outside the summerhouse, Eloise busy drawing, and Anna chatting or reading or sorting pebbles or eating apples. Anna never seemed to notice or mind that Eloise didn't talk; Anna chattered enough for both of them.

Nearly always, the first thing Eloise did when she arrived was to dive into the silvery water of the pool. She'd swim while Anna watched, but Anna never swam. Eloise couldn't understand why; if *she* owned a glorious pool like this, she'd swim every day. She held out her hand to Anna, but Anna shook her head.

'I can't. It's too deep, I can't touch the bottom.'

So Eloise would haul herself out, dripping, and wrap herself in her sun-warmed towel.

Once or twice the girls had to hide in the summerhouse because 'the guests' wanted to use the swimming pool. They ducked out of sight, listening to the splashes and shrieks of the adults, while Anna stifled her giggles, and Eloise pulled silly faces to make it worse, until Anna slid sideways and cried with silent laughter. But the guests mostly used the pool in the evenings and at night, Anna said, because in the daytime they were working.

'You can't let anyone see you,' Anna insisted, and Eloise let herself be hidden; she didn't want to be seen, anyway.

One afternoon as Eloise rode down Mo's street, she saw someone in the next-door garden: not Tommy, but a bearded man in shabby clothes, kneeling by a flowerbed. He looked up as she swung round into the driveway, and raised his hand.

'Ah, you must be Mrs Mo's granddaughter.'

Eloise stopped the bike and looked at the ground. The bearded man advanced to the low dividing fence; he held out his hand to shake hers, then dusted it on his trousers.

'Excuse me – gardening. Weeding, to be exact. It is strange, even with no rain, the weeds still flourish. Is it the same for you?'

Eloise stared at the ground.

'Well, it was a pleasure to meet you, Eloise,' said Tommy's dad, just as if they'd had a proper conversation. 'I am Dr Durrani. I was Professor Durrani, once upon a time. But not any more. That was my job – talking, talking all day, lectures and speeches and meetings.' He glanced around conspiratorially. 'May I tell you a secret? I am quite glad to have a rest from all that talk, talk, talk. Sometimes there is nothing to say, you know?' He grinned suddenly, splitting his neat beard in two, and Eloise found herself smiling back. He nodded. 'I thought you would agree with me. These days, I am better at listening. You understand?'

Eloise gave a nod.

'Yes. I think you are good at listening too, and watching. It's all in here, hmm?' He gently tapped the side of his head. 'This is what some people do not understand. They think if nothing comes out of the mouth, there is nothing in the mind. All hollow, like a shell. No one inside.'

Eloise curled her fingers round the handlebars. Did he think there was nothing in *her* mind, because she never spoke? Was that what everyone thought?

'Some people might think it's easy to stop talking. You never have to choose, this or that; other people decide for you. The hollow shell floats on the waves, carried where the sea takes it.' His dark eyes smiled at Eloise, and his voice was kind. 'But the words are still there, like little fish, hiding inside. One day, when you need them, the fish will swim out.'

He smiled again, then politely stepped backward. 'Excuse me, Miss Eloise. I must continue with my weeding.'

He knelt again by the flowerbed, moving one leg with his hands as if it were rusted stiff. Eloise watched for a second, then she pushed her bike round the back of the house.

'So you've met Professor Durrani,' said Mo over their dinner of tinned soup. 'He's a clever man, a psychologist. You know what that is?'

Eloise knew. At her last school, when they finally worked out that she was always quiet, they'd sent her into a room with a psychologist, a woman in a blue jacket who'd asked lots of questions in a soothing voice and let them hang in the air while Eloise stared at the carpet.

But term had finished before they could arrange another meeting, and Dad had screwed up the letter from the school, thrown it in the bin and announced they were moving to the country.

Tommy's father wasn't like that woman. Everything about her had been fake: her careful voice, her artificial smile, the dye in her hair. But Tommy's dad seemed real; Eloise liked him. She didn't want him to think there was nothing in her mind, that she was empty and echoing like a seashell.

She didn't want Mo to think that either, or Anna, or Tommy.

As she cleaned her teeth that night, she looked at her reflection in the mirror. Was there anyone there? Suddenly she felt frightened. She spat out the toothpaste, banged the toothbrush on the basin, and made as much noise as she could, to prove to herself that she was still real.

Eloise dreamed she was swimming in the ocean, deep beneath the waves, in an emerald-lit landscape of flickering fish and towering coral. Far off in the distance, she saw a castle resting on the ocean floor – like a model in an aquarium. Tiny figures waved to her from the battlements and faint voices reached her through the water.

She began to swim toward them, but as she swam, the water thickened around her. Eloise kicked and pushed with all her strength, but she couldn't get any nearer to the castle. It wasn't a castle any more, it was a sunken boat.

Though she didn't seem to get any closer, she could see the little figures more clearly. Their voices were fainter now; they were turning away. She saw Dad and Bree and Mo and Tommy, except Tommy had a beard. And there was Anna, with her hands on her hips and her chin jutting up. Behind Anna was a woman, a grown-up woman, and Eloise knew it was her mother. Her mother was moving away, a blur of red and gold backing into the shadows; she was almost gone, and Eloise swam and kicked so hard she thought her lungs would burst, and she opened her mouth to scream out, *Mum! I'm coming, Mum!* But Anna was gone, Mum was gone, they were all drifting away, and Eloise's mouth filled with water, and she was choking, drowning, and no one could hear. She jerked awake into the dark, her heart pounding, and she couldn't get back to sleep.

The next morning was very hot. The radio said there were bushfires in the national park; the smoke gave the sky a bronze sheen. The radio also promised there'd be thunderstorms later, and hoped that rain would put out the fires. But Mo said it wouldn't rain, it never rained any more.

Even though she'd done it so often now, Eloise still held her breath as she stepped forward across the grass, eyes closed, into the mysterious silence that carried her into Anna's time. She wondered what it must look like to Anna, or anyone else who might be watching: a girl stepping out of the air, shimmering into being? Or a ghostly image that became solid, hardening into shape, like a trickle of wax?

In Anna's time, the sky was clouded over, and the air was still. Eloise hurried to the summerhouse, still haunted by her dream. She was half-afraid that Anna wouldn't be there, that she might have vanished away. But nothing could happen to Anna, she reminded herself; Anna's future was already decided. She would grow up and marry Stephen McCredie and have one baby girl, and name her Eloise . . .

If only there was some way to let her know how glad Eloise was to have found her, how precious this time was. If only there was some gift Eloise could give her.

Anna came running out of the summerhouse, bouncing like an excited puppy.

'I've had the most *splendufferous* idea!' Her eyes shone, and she tugged at Eloise's sleeve. 'Dad said we could only use white paint on the *outside* of the summerhouse. But he didn't say anything about the *inside*. Let's make it *jorgeous*! I've got paints, all different

colours, and brushes, and everything! Do you want
to help?'

Suddenly Eloise realised what her gift could be.
She took a deep breath. Then she whispered, 'Yes.'

8

'Hooray!' shouted Anna, though it wasn't clear whether she was excited about the painting or about Eloise finding a voice; maybe it was both. She dragged Eloise inside the summerhouse and showed her a treasure trove of paint tins, brushes, trays and buckets.

Eloise widened her eyes in a question.

'My mumma's,' said Anna. 'I snuck into her studio. She won't mind. We always do painting together. When she's here . . .' Anna's voice trailed off. 'I told you she was away, didn't I?'

'Yes,' whispered Eloise. Her voice was raspy with disuse.

Anna jammed a knife under a paint lid and prised

it up. 'She's gone away all summer. It's a prize or something. She's in America.'

Eloise cleared her throat. 'She's . . . an artist?' She'd never known her mother's mother was an artist; that explained where her own love of drawing must come from. It gave Eloise a warm feeling of belonging, as if this unknown grandmother had reached out of the past and wrapped her arms around her.

'I told you that already,' said Anna impatiently. 'Weren't you listening? What about this colour, what do you think?'

Eloise surveyed the array of paint pots. She whispered hesitantly, 'Want to . . . paint a picture?'

Anna's face lit up. 'Oh, yes! That'd be *mangificent*.' She snatched up a brush and danced around the summerhouse. 'Let's paint something *ginormous*. Let's paint something *fierce*!'

'A storm?' croaked Eloise.

'Yes, yes, a big black dark thunderstorm!' cried Anna, brandishing her brush like a weapon. 'That'll be fun!' She lunged for a big tin of black paint and wrestled the lid off so it spun clattering across the floor. She plunged the biggest brush into the dark paint and swept a stripe of black across one of the six blank walls of the summerhouse. She turned triumphantly to Eloise. 'Come on! You help too. You do the storm clouds.' She thrust the brush into Eloise's hand and seized another, smaller one, which she dipped into another paint pot. She streaked dark, bitter yellow down the neighbouring wall. 'Lightning!'

Eloise hung back as Anna swooped and darted, picking up a second brush and then a third, dragging swirls of brooding green and purple across the pale, blank wall. 'Come *on*!' cried Anna. 'You do some too!'

Eloise daubed some cautious black marks in a corner.

'More! Bigger! Darker!' Damp strands of hair clung to Anna's neck and forehead.

Eloise slapped on the black paint, thicker and darker, spreading black smudges of thundercloud across the walls. She swept her arm in wide arcs, bolder and bolder, slapping it over Anna's flickers of yellow and purple and green, blotting out the bright streaks with grim darkness.

'Your turn for yellow.' Anna thrust a dripping brush into Eloise's hand and seized the black brush from her. Now Eloise was painting over the black cloud-shapes with yellow, jumping to spread the paint in jagged strokes as high as the ceiling, shooting up onto the underside of the roof. Eloise had never painted like this before, outside the lines, wild and fierce and reckless. Anna danced about, laughing and sweating, and Eloise felt the sweat slide down her own back as she stretched and swished.

When they'd covered every bit of the two walls with paint, they stood back, panting for breath.

Anna slowly tilted her head, gazing up. Her forehead crinkled. 'It's horrible!' she wailed. 'It's dark, it's ugly! I hate it!'

She crumpled to the ground and buried her head in her arms. Awkwardly Eloise patted her shoulder. Then she put her arm around Anna and squeezed the small shaking figure. *I'm hugging my mum*, she told herself, and the black walls blurred as her own eyes filled with tears.

'I hate it. I hate it,' Anna sobbed. 'We've ruined everything!'

Eloise let out a hiccup of laughter.

'Don't *laugh*!' Anna pulled fiercely away. 'Don't laugh at me. It's not *funny*.'

Eloise sobered. 'We can fix it,' she whispered.

'How, how can we fix it? It's a *catstrophe*.'

'Paint . . . over it.'

Anna sat up. She sniffed, and wiped her face on her arm, considering. 'You think we can? Really?'

Eloise lifted her shoulders and let them fall.

And then all at once she was sitting among the dead leaves on the floor of the empty summerhouse. The sun was going down, and she was alone. She could smell smoke from the bushfires, and when she came out of the summerhouse, a smoky haze lay over the garden.

There had been no rain; the concrete around the empty pool was dry. But as Eloise pedalled home she heard the distant rumble of thunder over the hills, and lightning flashed, a thin metallic thread between earth and sky. *That's how we should have painted it*, thought Eloise, and she watched the horizon so intently that she almost wobbled off the road.

'Those Durranis have left us dinner again. Rice and chicken something.' Mo gave Eloise a sharp look. 'Are you all right? Not sunstruck? Maybe you should stay home tomorrow. You shouldn't be out exploring in all that smoke, anyway.'

Eloise made an effort to straighten up, and she shook her head vigorously.

'You are all right, aren't you?' said Mo. 'Made some friends? Got things to do?'

Eloise nodded firmly. The last thing she wanted was for Mo to forbid her to go out. And she *did* have a friend; she *did* have things to do.

But she was so exhausted that she went to bed straight after dinner and fell asleep the moment her head touched the pillow. In her dreams she heard the phone ring on and on, and the grumble of Mo's voice; then she dreamed someone touched her shoulder and murmured, 'Are you awake? Your father's on the phone.'

But Eloise just rolled over and pushed herself further into sleep, and she thought she heard another voice, a deep kindly voice, explaining that sometimes there was nothing to say.

The next day Mo was back at work on her book of sea voyages, tapping away in the study, and Eloise rode off again to the big house. The radio said the fires in the national park had been contained, but smoke haze still lingered over the town. Eloise could taste it in her throat.

Smoke lay over the garden like a dirty mist, tinting the sunlight orange. Eloise squeezed her eyes shut and tiptoed toward the summerhouse, her mind full of that other world.

As she came past the screen of trees and the raucous chorus of cicadas gave way to the buffer of silence, the smell of smoke lifted, replaced by the smell of fresh paint, and there was Anna, beaming, her clothes spattered with white.

'I found a *ginormous* tin of white paint,' she said at once. 'And a roller, look.' A huge paint roller, taller than Anna herself, was propped in one corner. Anna gave Eloise a little shove. 'You didn't come and help! You never come when it's a really big job, I had to do it all myself.'

Eloise peered around. 'It's gone.' The walls were blank again, but faintly grey, where the black paint still showed through.

'Why didn't you come? You haven't come for three whole days.'

How could one day in her time stretch to three

in Anna's? 'Sorry,' said Eloise helplessly. 'Can't help it.'

'Oh, never mind.' Anna bounded around the summerhouse. 'You're here now. What are we going to paint today?'

'A shipwreck,' said Eloise without thinking.

Anna clasped her hands. 'Oh, *yes*! How will we do it?'

Eloise stared around the summerhouse. The two walls where they'd painted the storm were still damp with white paint; better to use a different section. After a minute she sketched with her hands. 'The sea – storm at the back – and the ship there – and in the front . . .' She stopped.

'People drowning,' said Anna with relish. 'Where's your pencil? You better draw it on first.'

Eloise dragged the pencil across the walls, tentatively at first, then with growing confidence as Anna cheered her on. 'Um,' she said. 'Drowned people . . . next to a swimming pool?'

Anna laughed. 'I don't care. No one'll see it except us. This is *my* place. What's that?'

'Rocks,' said Eloise. 'To wreck the ship.'

'Can I do them?' begged Anna, and without

waiting for a reply, she grabbed a brush and began to dab the rocks into existence, filling Eloise's pencilled outline with streaks and blobs of brown.

Eloise painted the ship. It was a white ocean liner with red funnels, like the one in the movie *Titanic*. Eloise painted it up on end, poised at the moment before it slid beneath the icy waves. She used the finest brush, tipped with black paint, for the tiny figures that spilled over the sides and into the water. Jab, jab, jab, she sent dozens of passengers to their doom.

'I can't *see* them,' complained Anna. 'Do bigger ones, up the front.'

Eloise sketched a face. Its mouth was open, its hair plastered to its skull, eyes squeezed shut. One hand clung to a rope that floated, useless, not attached to anything. The face could have belonged to a man or a woman; it was a blank face, a face of blind terror. Eloise's stomach felt cold, looking at it. A dead person. Dead, like her mother.

She looked across at Anna, busy dabbling green and blue to make the sea, her tongue sticking out of the corner of her mouth. It was impossible to believe that in Eloise's time, Anna wasn't alive, that there was no Anna.

Anna looked up, frowning. 'Don't stop,' she ordered. 'There's heaps to do yet.'

'Not stopping,' said Eloise.

She took up a thicker brush and began to swirl black and grey and white across the sky for the storm. The colours massed and congealed along the top of the summerhouse walls. Eloise stepped back. All that black was too heavy, it crushed the whole picture.

Eloise swapped to a thin brush and broke up the mass of darkness with the threads of white lightning she'd seen the night before. No, last night was in the future. She was in the past now. Safe in the past. Nothing could hurt her here, back here before she was born. This time was a safe place, the safest place there was . . .

There was too much lightning now. Eloise started to paint out the zigzag strands.

'No!' cried Anna. 'Leave it alone, you'll wreck it again!'

Eloise took a deep breath. Anna was right; fiddling always made things worse. She forced herself to dunk and wipe her brush. Anna needed help with all that sea.

Eloise mixed green and black into a murky colour,

and swept her brush up and across into wave-shapes. No, that looked all wrong – too smooth, too curvy, a friendly summer sea. She tried again. Choppy shapes, hard-edged, almost square. Much better. Now it was a scary sea, a sea you could easily drown in.

'Ooh, that's *splendufferous*!' cried Anna. 'How did you do that?'

Eloise showed her how to paint the shapes, then, suddenly inspired, she tipped the waves with a hard white edge of foam that echoed the white strands of lightning. *Yes*. This sea was vast, and cold. It would slap you in the face, grab your ankles and suck you under. This was an angry sea, a ruthless sea. It was overwhelming. No lifeboat, no oars could save you from this sea; nothing could.

Eloise lowered her brush and shivered. For a second she thought she might faint.

Anna said, 'You've stopped again.'

Eloise dropped her brush into the bucket. 'Don't want to . . . paint any more.'

'You're a lazy slug,' said Anna, but she looked tired too; there were dark rings under her eyes. Neither of them had remembered to eat all day.

Anna rummaged in her pocket and pulled out

a jelly snake, dusted with lint. She offered it to Eloise, who shook her head.

They stood side by side in front of the picture they'd made together: the black slab of sky, the choppy blocks of sea, the rocks. The toy-like ship, seesawing in the air as the black dots of people rained down. The single pale ghost face, floating blind as a jellyfish, open-mouthed in the unfinished sea, clutching its hopeless loop of rope.

'No,' said Eloise. 'No.'

'I don't like it either.' Anna stuck one end of the snake in her mouth and chewed. 'It's *respulsive*.'

'Have to start again.'

'Paint it all over again?' Anna sagged. 'Will you come back tomorrow? Do you promise?'

Eloise said wretchedly, 'I'll try . . .'

But she was speaking to empty air, and a blank set of walls. The wave of time had swept her up and dumped her back on her own shoreline again, and she was all alone.

9

Eloise slid the plug into the bath and turned on the shower. It was hard to believe that not long ago, she would have just let the water pour away down the drain, that she hadn't known how precious water was. Bree used to have twenty-minute showers. Eloise could imagine how Mo would have thumped on the door and yelled at her.

Precious, beautiful water . . . She'd really like a swim today . . .

Suddenly she wrenched off the taps and jumped out of the bath.

She was barely dry, still buttoning her shorts, as she snatched some toast and crunched it down.

'You're in a hurry today.' Mo stared over the top of her glasses. 'Something urgent to do?'

Eloise nodded, then, as she passed Mo's chair, she impulsively dropped a kiss on her grandmother's wiry tangle of hair.

'Strewth! What's brought this on?' Mo looked up, startled. 'Not going to do anything silly, are you?'

Eloise shook her head and grinned as she flew out of the kitchen. She rushed out the back door, launched herself onto the bike and down the driveway, and nearly knocked over Tommy and a slightly-built woman in a blue headscarf as they stepped out onto the pavement.

'Watch it!' Tommy shouted after her, jolted out of his usual politeness, and Eloise glanced back to make sure they were all right. That must be Tommy's mum, the doctor. But she couldn't stop, not even for mothers; nothing could stop her today.

The smoke had dispersed and the air was clear. Eloise rode the short way, along the main street and past the shops, even though that hill was steeper. She pedalled down the road and through the sagging gates, along the rutted driveway and across the gravel. She was in such a hurry that she didn't drop the bike at the steps, but rode right around the house and through the tangled grass all the way to the summerhouse.

Let Anna be there. Let Anna be there, she prayed. She couldn't waste this idea. It filled up her head, she *had* to paint it. If only she could get it right.

She wobbled desperately past the screening trees, jumped off the bike and leapt through the silence into the other time.

'You nearly knocked me over!' shouted Anna indignantly.

'I know what to paint today!' burst Eloise. 'Better than yesterday—'

'Yesterday? That was *days* ago. I've been waiting and waiting, every day, and you never came! Don't you want to be my friend any more?'

Of course I do, Eloise tried to say, but her voice clogged her throat. She stared at Anna, mute and miserable, and Anna stared miserably back.

Then Anna underwent one of her sudden transformations. 'Oh, let's not fight, you're here now.'

'I *try* to come every day,' whispered Eloise unhappily.

'What do you mean? Why don't you just come? Does someone stop you? Do they lock you up?'

'No . . . but . . .' Eloise stopped. How could she explain to Anna who she was and where she came from? How could anyone handle a glimpse into her own future – a future where she was no longer alive? Eloise could never tell her, never.

'I'm sorry,' she said softly. 'I come as often as I can. Promise.'

'Okay,' mumbled Anna. 'I just get lonely, that's all.' Her eyes filled with those sudden tears that seemed to rise and fall like the tide, and she said, 'I miss my mumma.'

'Me too,' whispered Eloise. 'Me too.'

The two girls were silent, their loneliness wrapped around them like a dark mist. Eloise stared at the ground, a lump pressing inside her throat.

'Where's your mum, then?' Anna said in a small voice.

Eloise swallowed. 'She died.'

Anna's eyes went completely round. 'Oh . . . oh, no. What happened?'

'It was a car crash.' Eloise felt her voice scratching as she spoke. 'She didn't feel anything. It was instant.'

Her scalp prickled; she'd never told anyone about Mum's accident. She shouldn't be telling Anna now; surely it was wrong tell someone about their own death, even if they didn't know it . . . She grabbed up her pencil. 'Wait, see my idea,' she said hurriedly. 'Look at this.'

She swept the pencil across the pale expanse of the two walls they hadn't painted on yet, the two walls that faced the doorway and had clear light falling across them. She had to pin down her idea while she could still see it; the image had come to her so clearly in the shower, all in one piece, perfect.

Anna watched as Eloise sketched and paused and looked and sketched some more, lines of firm grey pencil laid over the pale boards, a picture emerging out of nothing.

'It's a girl. A girl flying? Ooh no, I see now. Is she swimming?'

'She's inside the ship.' Eloise's hand swooped over the wall. It was hard to get the scale right across the angle of the two walls; the girl's head was the wrong size. Impatiently she rubbed it out and tried again. 'She's under the water.'

'Drowned?' asked Anna ghoulishly.

'No, no – maybe – I don't think so.'

Eloise kept drawing. She wasn't sure about the edges of the picture, but the central image was strong and clear: the swimming girl, hair streaming in the water, bare feet kicking behind her.

'What's she holding?' Anna stepped in close to stare. 'Is it a mirror? A painting? Something in a frame.'

The girl held it out in front of her with one hand, as if she were about to swim right through the frame. Eloise scribbled, stood back, erased, scribbled again. She couldn't make the angle work.

'That hand looks all wrong,' said Anna helpfully.

'I know!' snapped Eloise.

'Look,' said Anna. 'Why don't you draw me?' Carefully she posed her hand, angling her fingers backward, and turned her big hopeful eyes to Eloise.

'Yes!' breathed Eloise. 'That's it . . .' She nudged Anna's hand into the right position, and sketched a few surer strokes on the wall.

The girl wasn't holding a mirror; it was a window. And through the window you could see – Eloise saw it clearly, all the edges sunlit and precise, not like the dreamy underwater shadows the girl swam through – you could see a garden. Eloise roughed in the outlines of the trees, the border of the flowerbeds, and the house behind, just enough to hint at the shapes, for later. Then she threw the pencil down and rushed for the paint tins.

Green and blue, a touch of red, to turn it murky purple. The colours swirled and blended. More green, dark green. Eloise dabbed it on the wall.

'Let me, let me!' Anna pleaded, jumping up and down behind her. 'I can do that. You do the girl.'

It was hard to paint someone swimming, suspended in water. How to show that her dress floated around her? Her hair waved delicately, like weeds in water. She was swimming away from the viewer; you could see the soles of her bare feet but not her face. One hand pointed backward, pale fingers like – like little fish. Yes, she was too pink, too pink! Feverishly Eloise mixed colours. She should be silvery, like a fish. That grey was too dark. A splodge of white, mix it in. Yes, that was almost right. A touch of yellow. And white, tinged with blue, for her dress. And her hair greeny-dark, seaweed-dark.

'You have to keep swimming through.' Anna's dark head was bent with concentration as her brush swished and dotted. 'That's what my mumma always says. Never give up.'

Swimming through. Swimming through life, toward the light and the garden. Eloise liked the sound of that.

Colour exploded from her brush; with every touch, the picture flowered and swarmed into being. From Eloise's imagination, it zinged through her hand and her brush and onto the wall, becoming something real. This morning it had been just an idea trapped inside Eloise's head; now it was free, something new and fresh, and anyone could see it. *Making something*: it was the best feeling in the world.

Steadily Anna filled in the background. A pale green shape. Dark lines, shadowy forms. It wasn't until Eloise stood back that she realised what Anna had done. It was the house – inside the house. The lines were a little wobbly, the colours uncertain, but Eloise could see the staircase, the double doors, the glass panels. Anna had painted the inside of her own house, sunk to the bottom of the sea.

She and Eloise looked at each other and laughed, as if it were a joke they'd made together.

Now Eloise helped her: a school of tiny fish darted

through the doorway to the living room; a drowned table floated; an upturned vase spilled flowers that drifted in the water. The stairs curved up and away, the thin line of the railing just visible in the shadows.

A shiver ran over Eloise's scalp as she saw that the girl she'd painted was the same girl she'd seen on her very first day, the girl who'd run down the steps and turned to stare. It was Anna, of course, a stranger then, but so familiar now . . . and then she saw what was wrong with the girl's other hand: it should be curled around the frame, *pulling* her through.

Eloise sprang to fix it, and at once she was lost again inside the picture. It filled her whole mind; it *was* her whole mind. Nothing else existed but the paints and brushes, the shapes and colours, the balance of light and dark, her hand and her eyes. She dodged and danced, crouched and stretched, not even aware of her own movements until she paused to gulp from her water bottle and realised that her muscles ached and her eyes were sore. But there was still the garden to finish yet.

Eloise stood close to the wall and squinted, the finest brush in her hand as she worked on the bright square inside the frame. Yellow and white, the palest green; the whole house just visible in the background, tall trees with sunshine dazzling off their leaves, bushes studded with golden flowers. A window to another world, the whole *point* to the painting.

The house was inside the picture, and outside it. The house had turned inside out, the same way time had turned inside out, folding Eloise into the past and shaking her out again into the present.

'I'm tired,' groaned Anna, and flung herself down.

'Mm,' said Eloise. Just a shimmer of bright blue sky beyond the roof . . .

'Sit with me.' The edge of a whine in Anna's voice showed how tired she was. 'You can finish that later.'

'Mm . . .'

Anna unfolded herself and planted her fists on her hips. 'Come *outside*. It's too dark in here. Come out in the *sun*.'

Anna was right; the sun had swung around, it was almost too dark to see. Eloise dropped her brush into the water jar with a sigh, and stepped back to look at the picture.

It was finished. And it was good. It was better than good.

Eloise felt a wide smile stretch across her face. It wasn't perfect, but it *worked*. It was the first time she'd made something that matched, or almost matched, the idea in her head; it was the first time she'd ever wanted to show off something she'd painted. She felt as if her chest would burst. She wanted everyone in the world to see it.

But Anna had seen it. Her mother had seen a picture that Eloise had painted, a good picture, maybe the first really good picture she'd ever made. Even if no one else in the world ever looked at it, that was something.

Eloise flung her arms into the air and whooped for joy. Anna whooped, too – not quite as elated as Eloise but prepared to be carried along by Eloise's delight. Eloise grabbed Anna's hands and swung her around, out into the afternoon sunshine and danced her around the pool. 'It's done, it's done!' she sang, and then she threw Anna's hands away, spun a pirouette and jumped into the pool, clothes and all.

She heard Anna shriek, and then a tremendous splash, and Anna was in the water too, almost on top of her, screaming and spluttering. Eloise ducked away. Anna thrashed and gasped, churning the water desperately till she reached the side and clung there by her fingertips. 'Oh!' she gasped, breathless. 'That was *fun*!'

'I thought you were drowning!' shouted Eloise, and splashed her, and Anna splashed back, and they both screamed and ducked and splashed again, dragged down by their wet clothes, until they were breathless.

Eloise swam over and rested her arms on the side of the pool beside Anna.

Anna pushed herself away into the water by her fingertips and pulled herself in again. Suddenly she said, 'What's your name?'

'Eloise.'

'Eloise?' repeated Anna blankly. Her face changed. She said again, 'Eloise', carefully, as if she were tasting it. She gave a solemn nod.

Eloise hadn't really realised that Anna didn't know her name; all this time, she'd never asked.

Suddenly Anna smiled into Eloise's face. 'Eloise!' she sang. 'Will you teach me how to swim?'

'Okay,' said Eloise, and she splashed Anna in the face again. Anna screamed and ducked away.

Neither of them noticed the tall man standing by the pool's side, his face dark with anger.

'Anna. *Anna!*'

Both girls looked round, struck dumb with shock.

'What the *hell* do you think you're doing? Get out of the pool right now.'

'Dad—' Anna faltered. But she clutched at the edge and tried to haul herself out. Her father grabbed her wrist and yanked her roughly from the water.

'How many times?' He was shaking her. 'How many times have we told you *not* to go swimming alone?'

'But Dad, I'm not—' stuttered Anna.

Eloise trod water, her heart pounding. Anna's dad glared at Anna, then swept his furious gaze all around the pool, across Eloise and back to Anna. He shook her again.

'What rubbish is this now? There's no one here but you.'

10

Anna's eyes widened in shock. Her father wrapped her roughly in a towel and rubbed her hair as if she were a much younger child. She craned to look past him, to reassure herself that Eloise was still there in the water.

'Dad, look – she is – she really is—' Anna choked.

'*Enough!*' Some words exploded from him, in a language Eloise didn't recognise. Anna looked scared; she huddled away from him, cowering beneath the towel.

Eloise felt her own face go numb, her own mouth sag open. It was plain that Anna's father – her own grandfather, the grandfather she had never met –

simply could not see Eloise there in the middle of the pool. He couldn't see her.

Eloise found she could move, though her arms and legs were heavy. She dragged herself slowly to the edge of the pool. She could hear her own voice, shrill and uncertain. 'It's okay. I wouldn't let her drown. I was watching her . . .'

But Anna's father spoke over the top of her. He didn't hear Eloise; he couldn't see her and he couldn't hear her. He put his hands on Anna's shoulders and knelt to look into her face. 'This is not funny any more, baby. This is dangerous now. So many times we told you, you can play in the summerhouse if you promise – *promise* – not to go into the pool when no one else is there. And now look at this.'

'I'm *not* a baby.' Anna pressed her lips together. 'And she *is* here. I can see her.'

'This imaginary friend of yours? Yes, I heard you talking about all the paintings you do together, the games you play, I heard you. But Anna, you know it's not real. You know that, don't you?'

Anna said nothing. She flicked a glance over her father's shoulder to Eloise, who still clung to the side of the pool. She pressed her lips together even harder, and blinked.

Anna's father put his arm around her shoulder. 'Come up to the house now, you're shivering. This is my fault. I shouldn't let you be so much by yourself. I'm sorry for shouting, baby, but you have to understand . . .'

Still talking earnestly, he drew Anna away from the pool, through the gate in the fence, around the trees and up the slope toward the house. Anna walked with her head bowed, saying nothing, her bare feet speckled with grass clippings.

Eloise's teeth chattered. She gripped the edge of the pool and tried to pull herself out, but she sank back, as if all the strength had drained out of her arms. She heaved again and rolled out of the water, and lay for a moment on the wet concrete, shivering. At last she managed to crawl into the summerhouse and find her towel. What would Anna's father have said about the paintings on the walls? Would he think Anna had done them all by herself? Or would they be invisible to him, too?

Eloise wished she could forget how it had felt when her grandfather's eyes raked past her, unseeing, but she couldn't forget it.

When she'd dried herself as best she could, she put on her hat and backpack and stood in the middle of the dark summerhouse with her hands limp at her sides. It was the first time she'd ever wanted to go home before the time-wave rushed to sweep her away, the first time she'd stood there, helpless, waiting.

Outside it was twilight, and the indigo ink of night gradually darkened the sky. Eloise could see a single star. She left the summerhouse and the pool enclosure and walked around the screen of trees, where Anna had gone. Golden light streamed down the slope from the big house, remote as a lighthouse, as far away as another country. Slowly Eloise retraced her path, trying to walk back into her own time; she almost thought she could feel the dense shimmering wall between her time and the other, resistant against her skin. If only she could hold up a window, like the girl in the painting, and swim through it . . .

Keep swimming through, she thought. *You have to keep swimming through. Don't give up.* And so she walked steadily on, up the slope and back again, invisible inside the gathering dusk, listening to the murmur of music and conversation and the clink of plates and glasses from the open windows of the big house, until at last, at last, the welcome silence rushed over her and towed her away.

Dusk was falling in her own time, too, but it was still hot. The setting sun splashed vivid orange light on the bare planks of the summerhouse walls. There were no paintings, no trace of paint. Someone must have painted over them, between Anna's time and now. Dead leaves littered the floor.

Eloise's shoulders drooped as she picked up her bike where it had fallen. *Swimming through.* Her clothes were still damp and sticky, clinging to her skin. The cicadas were so loud it was hard to even think. She pushed the bike along the dark tunnel of the driveway and wobbled out onto the road. If only swimming through didn't make you so very tired . . .

One foot down, and then the other, she pushed the bike toward home.

Eloise was inside the back door before she realised that Mo had visitors. She caught the door before it banged shut and eased it silently closed, then she stood still, on tiptoe, listening.

No one had heard her come in; they were all talking at once. Mo was saying, 'When she's ready—'

Tommy's excited voice cut in. 'But my father can help her!'

Then the gentle tones of Tommy's dad. 'It is not appropriate, Osman.'

'But then everyone can see how clever you are!' cried Tommy. 'We have to show them. Everyone will come to you!'

'You can't help someone who isn't ready to be helped,' said Mo dryly. 'No matter how clever you are. No offence, Professor.'

'None taken, I assure you. I apologise for my son, who seems to believe I should demonstrate my skills to the town by practising on the neighbours.'

'Only some of the neighbours,' muttered Tommy.

Mo said sharply, 'I hope you're not suggesting your father should brush up his skills on *me*.'

There was an awkward silence, then Tommy said, subdued, 'Of course not, Mrs Mo. I'm sorry, Mrs Mo.'

Mo snorted.

'Forgive us, Mrs Mo,' said Tommy's dad. 'We have trespassed on your time for long enough.' He said something to Tommy in their own language, and

Eloise heard them get up to go. She waited, holding her breath, as they all moved out into the hallway.

'Thank you for the curry,' said Mo gruffly. 'Again.'

'Not at all. Leisure in which to cook has proved to be an unexpected benefit of unemployment.'

'And you cheer up, Tommy. You look like you've lost a shilling and found sixpence.'

'I beg your pardon, Mrs Mo?'

'Never mind. I know you meant well. But when Eloise and I are ready for help, we'll ask for it, all right? Till that day comes you can mind your own beeswax.'

'I don't understand, Mrs Mo.'

'Oh, forget it. Buzz off. See you later. Goodbye, Professor.'

Eloise heard the door slam shut, then open again. Mo called out through the screen, 'Thank you!'

Eloise quickly changed her clothes, threw the wet ones into the laundry basket, and crept silently into the kitchen where a covered casserole dish sat on the table. Mo came marching in, and jumped at the sight of her.

'Scared the living daylights out of me! What are

you, a ghost? Where the devil have you been? It's nearly dark.'

Eloise shrugged and spread her hands in apology.

'You just missed Tommy and his father. They brought round another curry. Lamb this time, I think they said.'

Eloise nodded, non-committal, though she saw Mo glance swiftly at her as if trying to guess whether she'd heard any of their conversation.

As she and Mo ate dinner, Eloise thought about what she had overheard. It had startled her when Mo had lumped the two of them together as needing help – or rather, not needing it, thanks very much.

Eloise was glad. All she wanted was to be left alone, that was all she had ever wanted.

But then she remembered that horrible sensation when Anna's dad had looked through her, spoken through her, as if she didn't exist. In the other time, Eloise was a ghost – except to Anna . . .

And, Eloise realised, she was as good as a ghost in her own time, too: silent, invisible, sidling out of rooms. Maybe Mo was wrong. Maybe she did need help, after all. Her throat tightened.

Mo asked her suddenly, 'You're all right, aren't you? Getting along? Finding enough to do?'

Eloise nodded. She could speak to Anna, but she couldn't speak to Mo – not yet. Her hands were still spattered with grey and green and white paint. She wondered if Mo would ask what she'd been doing, but she didn't.

As Eloise picked the paint from under her fingernails, she reflected that Mo wasn't very good at noticing. Either that or she was extra good at pretending not to.

'Your father rang today.' Mo dropped the serving spoon back into the casserole dish. 'Says he'll be here on Christmas Eve.' She looked at Eloise sharply. 'You know it's Christmas next week, don't you? On Tuesday?'

Eloise chewed slowly. She had no idea what day it was.

'Today's Saturday, by the way,' said Mo dryly. 'You need money? For presents?'

Eloise paused, then, inspired, she shook her head. She could give them drawings: one for Mo and one for Dad. She could do that by Tuesday, easily. Dad would have a picture of the house, of course. And for

Mo she could copy the summerhouse painting – the girl swimming through the window. Yes, she was sure Mo would like that . . .

But what about Anna?

Time ran at a different, faster speed for Anna; perhaps she'd already had her Christmas. But Eloise wanted to give her a present too, especially after what had happened today. After all, it was Eloise's fault that her father had growled at her.

She shovelled up the last of her rice and curry and slid from the table.

'Don't suppose there's any point asking what you want?' asked Mo abruptly. 'Books? A camera? Think I got my first camera when I was about your age. Paints?'

Eloise nodded eagerly to the last. But it wasn't till she was seated cross-legged on her island bed, sketching, that she realised that Mo would have to ask the Durranis to buy her present for her. It was weird to think of Tommy, or his father, who she barely knew, shopping for her Christmas present.

Then another thought struck her. She tore a page from her sketchbook and wrote a laborious note.

When she knocked on Mo's door, the noise of

typing broke off into a startled silence. Eloise knocked again.

'Come in then, don't stand there like a stunned mullet,' came Mo's impatient voice.

Eloise pushed open the door. It was the first time she'd ever been inside Mo's study. It was stuffy and airless, and an old-fashioned fan whirred on the floor, riffling sheaves of paper on Mo's desk as it rotated. The desk was under the window, the computer propped on a stack of books. Mo swung around in her chair. Her hair was wild, as if she'd been digging her hands through it. One pair of glasses rested on her head, one pair at the end of her nose and a third dangled round her neck. She glared at Eloise. 'Don't you remember rule number one? What's the matter?'

Mutely Eloise handed her the note.

Mo squinted at Eloise's terrible handwriting, '*Do you want me to buy presents for the Next Doors?*' She grimaced at Eloise. 'Not game to spell Durrani, eh? Don't blame you.' She folded the paper, gazing at Eloise over her glasses. 'There's no need for that. I've asked your father to take care of it, as a matter of fact. But thank you for asking. It was . . . thoughtful.'

Eloise stared at the carpet. The fan whirred around and lifted the hair on her forehead.

'All right,' said Mo. 'My sea voyages are calling. Buzz off.'

Eloise withdrew, and a minute later the clackety-clack of the computer keyboard started up again on the far side of the door. Would she get to read Mo's book one day? Eloise wondered if Mo would ever finish it.

11

The next day, Eloise crept toward the summerhouse. She was almost too nervous to close her eyes, scared that the magic wouldn't work. Last night it had seemed harder to push back into her own time; perhaps it would be harder to get through into Anna's time today. She walked forward, into the red dark behind her eyelids, through the shrilling of the cicadas. Then the rush of silence washed over her.

When she opened her eyes, she was in the other time, with the neat summerhouse, the white fence, the cropped lawn. Someone had abandoned a blanket and a book in the middle of the grass. The swimming pool glimmered, diamond-bright in the early morning sunlight. Birds shouted from every corner of the garden, and the tips of the trees were dipped in gold.

Eloise hurried into the summerhouse. She knew just what she wanted to do for Anna's present. It was only a small present; maybe Anna wouldn't even notice it. But Eloise would know.

She looked at the painting of the swimming girl and her heart expanded. It *was* good. The swimming girl was fluid as a mermaid, but there was nothing watery about her: she was firm and full of energy. And now Eloise picked up a brush to add the final touch to the picture.

Inside the bright square of garden she painted a tiny figure: another girl, in a big hat, holding up one hand in a wave of greeting. She didn't sketch it first, just dabbed it directly into the heart of the painting, a solitary small dark shadow in the sunlit garden, dark inside light inside dark, just as the dark painting was folded inside the bright summerhouse.

The two painted girls held out their hands to each other, across the frame that joined and separated them, across the light of the garden and the dark underwater, the garden girl in her dark frock and the swimming girl in her pale nightgown. And if they were both Anna, it didn't matter; it was as if a dream Anna waved to the real Anna, though Eloise wasn't sure which was which . . .

Anna.

Eloise put down her brush. Anna wasn't here. As slowly as possible, she washed her brush, tidied the paints, took a drink from her water bottle. But still Anna didn't come.

Eloise told herself that it was still early; there was plenty of time. But she knew, somehow, that Anna wasn't going to come.

She took a deep breath and ducked out of the summerhouse. Then, without letting herself hesitate, she set off round the side of the swimming pool, along Anna's secret path through the bushes toward the house.

She kept her head down. The usual noises wafted from the house: a repeated phrase from a piano, someone laughing, a door banging shut. It was so strange to think of the deserted, derelict house she'd seen that first day with Dad full of people and furniture and music.

She lurked by the back door. Anna's father

couldn't see or hear her, but maybe other people could. And even if they couldn't, she didn't want to experience that horrible feeling when they looked straight through her. Eloise waited till the clatter from the kitchen fell silent, then she pushed the door open a crack and slipped inside.

The back hallway was empty. There was the same green-felt door, but the felt was bright and new, and the studs that nailed it in place were shining. Eloise pushed through it into the foyer. The piano noise came clearly from one of the big rooms. Everything looked lighter, brighter, with fresh white paint, vases of flowers, bright canvases on the walls.

Eloise ran on tiptoe across the foyer and up the curving stairs. She'd never been upstairs before. She felt light-headed, almost queasy. Inside the house, she had a feeling that she'd never had in the garden or the summerhouse: that she was in the wrong place, that she didn't belong here.

Three corridors led in different directions. Down one of them she heard a buzz of voices; she veered away. Anna had said she could see the summerhouse from her bedroom. So her room must be on this side of the house—

Eloise risked calling in a whisper, 'Anna?'

A door clicked open, and a high, excited voice hissed, 'I'm here!'

Eloise dived inside and Anna instantly slammed the door behind her. 'Oh, I'm so glad you're here!' Anna's cheeks were flushed, and her eyes were huge and shiny. She threw her arms round Eloise and squeezed her tight.

Eloise had a confused impression of overflowing bookshelves, drawers yanked open, an old-fashioned white bedstead with the covers tossed about. The next instant Anna released her.

'I was starting to think I *had* imagined you. But I didn't, did I? You're as real as me.'

'We're as real as each other,' Eloise assured her, but as she spoke she felt giddy again. Were they real? Were they dreaming? If she belonged in Anna's future, should she be here now? Suppose Anna suddenly decided not to have any children, would Eloise vanish, like a shadow when the torch clicks off?

'Dad's so upset with me. He says I'm too old for imaginary friends and he says I'm not even allowed to go to the summerhouse on my own . . . He rang

Mumma in America and she was nearly going to come home.' Tears poured down Anna's cheeks. 'I miss you so much,' she wept. 'You've been away so long.'

Eloise felt stricken. She didn't know what to do. 'I can't help it,' she whispered. 'It's not my fault.' She put her arms around Anna and hugged her. Anna smelled of soap and toast.

'I want to come with you,' sobbed Anna. 'I want to go to your place.'

Eloise stiffened. 'I don't know if you *can*.'

'Where is it, where you come from? It's a different time, isn't it?' She pulled away and gazed solemnly at Eloise. 'Are you dead? Is that why you came?'

'No!' said Eloise. 'I'm not dead.'

'Are you sure?'

'Of course I'm sure,' said Eloise uncertainly. 'Anyway, if I was dead, you couldn't come with me.'

'I could die too. Then we'd be together all the time.'

'No!' said Eloise in horror. 'Oh, no, you can't do that! And I'm *not* dead.'

'Dead people never think they're dead,' said Anna matter-of-factly, dabbing at her eyes. 'But if you're really not dead, you must come from the olden days.

Do you come from the olden days? Why can't I go back with you?'

'Because . . .' stammered Eloise. 'If you're not here . . . You just can't.'

'If I came into your time, I could be invisible like you,' said Anna. 'Is it fun being invisible?'

'No,' said Eloise. 'It's horrible.'

Anna stuck out her bottom lip. 'I still want to come. I want to see what the olden days are like. I want to stay there for a while, with you. I want to give Dad a big *fright*.'

'You can't,' said Eloise urgently. 'Anna, you can't do that. You have to stay here, with your dad. He'd go crazy if anything happened to you. The only reason he got so upset is because he was so worried. He doesn't want anything bad to happen to you, you're the most important thing—' She broke off. Suddenly she knew it was true. To Anna's dad, Anna was the most important thing in the whole world.

Eloise knew that she wasn't the most important thing to her father. Lots of things were more important than she was: work, projects, convention centres, girlfriends, money, cars, running away from everything that possibly reminded him of Mum.

Maybe Eloise reminded him of Mum. Maybe he was running away from her as well . . .

'I have to go,' she stammered. She felt peculiar, insubstantial, as if she really were a ghost, as if she might float up to the ceiling. She shouldn't be here; she couldn't stay any longer. 'Goodbye, Anna.'

She bolted from the room and ran down the hallway. It seemed that her feet skimmed along the blue-and-brown rug almost without touching it. Was she fading away? What if she was trapped here, a half-person, visible only to Anna? She heard voices; two people were walking up the stairs. Eloise skidded to a halt, but they didn't turn their heads; they walked past without seeing her.

'Wait!' Anna called behind her. 'Stay!'

The couple at the top of the stairs swung round toward her, startled.

'I can't!' cried Eloise in a burst of panic. 'I have to get home!'

The guests stared straight past her, unhearing. Eloise leapt down the stairs and tore across the foyer; she had to swerve around a woman in a print dress who didn't pause or step out of her way, but just kept walking.

Sobbing for breath, Eloise burst out into the sunlit garden and sprinted across the clipped grass. She didn't know if Anna had followed her; all she wanted was to escape back to her own time.

Eloise shut her eyes as she ran and held out her hands blindly before her. *Please, let me get home.* She ran and tripped and fell, the wind knocked out of her.

Fighting for breath, she stared up at the sky. Whether it was her own time or Anna's time, the sky was always the same, stretched tight as a canvas, flecked with cloud. Silence settled around her, soft as moth wings. The pain in her chest faded; she could breathe again. She sat up.

She was back in her own time. The grass rose high around her. The wild garden shrilled with the noise of cicadas, and the summerhouse sagged beneath its blanket of ivy. Eloise hid her face in her hands and began to cry.

12

'**E**l Dorado! Sweetheart!' Dad twisted round in his chair and pulled her into a hug. 'How are you, precious girl? Crikey, I've missed you! C'mere and give me a cuddle.'

Eloise threw her arms around him. He did care after all. He'd come early to surprise her. He was the best dad in the world.

Then, looking over the top of Dad's curly head, she saw a strange woman perched on the edge of Mo's hard green nubbly couch. Her blonde hair was brushed carefully to frame her face, which was as stiff and shiny as a mask. Her puffed-out lips half-smiled, but her eyes didn't. She wore a grey business suit, high heels and pale pink nail polish, and she held her champagne glass with the very tips of her fingers. Several bottles of champagne sat on the coffee table.

'Lorelei, this is my darling daughter, Eloise,' said Dad, squeezing Eloise so tightly round the waist she could hardly breathe. He said solemnly, 'Eloquence, I'd like you to meet a very important person. This is Lorelei Swan.'

'Hi,' said the woman coolly.

Eloise stared at her. She felt her own face stiffen into a cold mask that matched Lorelei Swan's.

'My little Electric Fence is a bit slow to warm up.' Dad gave Eloise a playful nudge. 'Don't mind her . . . Hey, hey, guess what? Lorelei's going to help us build our dream. What a pal, eh. What a sensible *investor*, I should say!' Dad's big laugh rang out.

Eloise and Lorelei Swan looked at one another. Lorelei Swan took a tiny sip of champagne, and her puffy mouth moved slightly in a tight, brief smile.

'Let's not get too carried away, Stephen,' she said. 'The deal's not done yet. Photos are all very well, but I still need to see the site.'

'Of course, of course!' Dad leapt up, releasing

Eloise so suddenly she nearly fell over. 'Let's go! What are we waiting for? Wanna come along, Elementary-my-dear-Watson?' Dad hiccupped.

Eloise shook her head. She didn't want to go anywhere with that woman, especially not to the house. Eloise and her dad's girlfriends usually didn't think much of each other, and she could already see this Lorelei Swan would be no exception.

'I'd better drive, don't you think?' Lorelei Swan plucked the car keys from Dad's hand.

Eloise had seen the big polished midnight-blue four-wheel drive parked out in the street, though she hadn't realised it was Dad's. Maybe it belonged to Lorelei Swan. She wondered what had happened to the little red sports car.

'—drop our bags at the hotel,' Dad was saying. 'Hey, Mo!' he yelled. 'Not expecting us back here for dinner, are you?'

Mo poked her head from the study. She must have been hiding in there all the time. 'How could I be?' she said sharply. 'Since I wasn't warned that you were coming, let alone bringing a guest.' She glared at Lorelei Swan.

''s all right, 's all right.' Dad raised his hands

placatingly. 'S'posed to be a good restaurant in Bungaree, might try that tonight. What do you think, Lorelei?'

'Sounds wonderful.' Lorelei Swan held out her hand to Mo. 'Lovely to meet you, Mrs McCredie.'

'Delighted,' said Mo, not shaking.

'Lovely to meet you, too, Eloise.' Lorelei Swan smiled her tight smile. 'I just know we're going to be the *best* of friends.'

Eloise didn't smile back. She and Mo moved together to the doorway and watched Dad and Lorelei Swan climb into the big blue four-wheel drive.

Mo called out, 'What about Christmas? You expecting Christmas dinner?'

Dad's window slid down. 'Course we are! Brought Lorelei all this way for a family Christmas, didn't I?'

Lorelei Swan said something inaudible, and Dad roared with laughter. The window slid up and the four-wheel drive blasted down the quiet street like a jet taking off.

'Your son?' came the gentle voice of Tommy's father. Eloise hadn't noticed him kneeling in the front garden, trowel in hand.

Mo snorted. 'My son and his latest floozy. And now he's gone and bloody invited her for Christmas dinner, what am I supposed to do about that?'

Tommy's father sat back on his heels and considered them both. 'Perhaps . . . I know Christmas is an important ritual, and I know how you dislike cooking. Perhaps my family could invite ourselves – if we might take such a liberty – and assist you in preparing the meal. But if you would prefer to spend the day in the company of your own family, naturally we would understand.'

Mo sniffed. 'Kind of you,' she said gruffly. 'Do hate cooking. Love you to come, actually, if you don't mind.'

Tommy's father's eyes twinkled. 'It would be an honour to share your holy day.'

'Not much holy about it these days. Just an excuse for spending money. But you'll be welcome. You'll be welcome.'

'Thank you.'

It occurred to Eloise, as she arranged her papers and pencils on her bed, that the Durranis really were very nice to Mo. She might do a picture for them, too.

But not for Lorelei Swan; *she* wasn't going to get a present. Eloise wondered if Anna had seen the addition to the summerhouse painting, or if she was still forbidden to go there. She felt bad about running away from Anna like that; next time she'd say sorry. She wouldn't be able to go to the house tomorrow; she'd have to work on her Christmas presents. Maybe she could take Anna a little present, too . . .

'Eloise.'

Eloise jumped. Mo was standing in the doorway.

'I was just going to say – you can use the table, you know. Kitchen, dining room, whatever. Spread yourself out. You don't have to stay locked away in here. This is your home, too.'

Eloise gazed up at her and nodded slightly.

'Good,' said Mo. 'Just as long as that's clear.'

She marched away and Eloise heard the study door slam.

Christmas Day dawned warm and muggy, with thunder in the air. The doorbell rang so early that Mo and Eloise were still in bed. When Mo opened the door, pulling her old tartan dressing-gown around her, the Durranis poured into the house in a warm and noisy flood. Bearing pots and dishes and boxes of food, they proceeded to take over the kitchen.

'Flaming invasion,' grumbled Mo. 'How am I supposed to make myself a cup of tea? Happy Christmas. Happy Christmas, Eloise,' she added, seeing her granddaughter peep round the doorway. 'Don't *hover*. You get on my nerves. Good luck reaching your Weetbix through this lot.'

'Quick, quick, Mrs Mo needs a cup of tea or she'll faint,' teased Tommy.

Eloise watched as Tommy's mother filled the kettle at the sink. She wore gold-rimmed spectacles and a purple headscarf. She was so slightly built that she seemed hardly bigger than Eloise, but her hands were strong. Eloise had only seen her once before, that brief glimpse in the street when she'd nearly run her and Tommy down.

'There's a present for you in the living room, Eloise,' said Mo. '*Yours* will be coming later,' she told the bustling Durranis. 'If my son's managed to do as he's told for once in his life.'

'Oh, Mrs Mo, that's not necessary.' Tommy's father waved a spoon in the air.

'Do you mind?' said Mo, but she was only pretending to be annoyed. Eloise could tell that underneath she was having a wonderful time.

In the living room, Eloise found an enormous parcel labelled with her name. Inside was a huge box filled with all kinds of paints: watercolours, tubes of oil, bottles of bright acrylic. She flew back to the kitchen and threw herself at Mo.

'Watch it, I'm an old lady you know,' Mo complained, but she hugged Eloise back. 'Anyway, you shouldn't be thanking me; it was this lot who did the shopping.'

'We didn't know what sort of paint you wanted,' said Tommy. 'So we went to the art shop in Bungaree and asked for one of everything.'

'No need to thank us,' said Tommy's mother softly. 'We can see that you like it.'

Shyly Eloise brought out her own presents: the copy of the swimming girl picture that she'd drawn for Mo, and the surprise present for the Durranis: a portrait of Tommy, which she handed to Tommy's mother, wishing Tommy wasn't there. She hadn't been able to think of any other picture they might like, but it was awkward to give it to them with Tommy standing right there.

The Durranis unwrapped the picture with cries of delight. Eloise had found some black cardboard at the back of Mo's linen cupboard to glue the drawings on, so they looked quite professional.

'It's wonderful, wonderful,' said Tommy's mother, and she gave Eloise such a warm smile that Eloise couldn't help smiling back.

'Thank you very much, Miss Eloise,' said Tommy's father solemnly.

'Made him look almost handsome.' Mo peered over their shoulders. 'You sure it's Tommy?'

Tommy made an embarrassed growling noise, which set off a fresh round of teasing. Eloise didn't dare look at him, but later in the day, when no one was watching, she saw him pick up the portrait and study it, and she thought he looked quite pleased.

'Good heavens,' said Mo when she'd pulled the wrapping off the swimming girl picture. She swapped her glasses and peered intently at the drawing. 'Good heavens,' she repeated softly, almost absently. 'It's the house, isn't it – inside the house? But that's the garden . . . Almost like Chagall, with that floating girl . . . You did this yourself, Eloise? Extraordinary.'

'She has a gift,' said Tommy's father. 'No doubt of it.'

They all looked at Eloise, even Tommy.

Then Tommy's mother laughed gently and put her arm around Eloise's shoulders. 'Enough! We are embarrassing the poor girl. Go, go.' She propelled Eloise toward the door. 'Wash and dress and we will have a beautiful breakfast waiting for you.'

'Breakfast as well!' cried Mo. 'Why don't you just go ahead and move in?'

Breakfast was delicious: warm bread with cherry jam, eggs and hot sweet tea. The Durranis laughed and joked and teased Mo, who grumbled and humphed, but laughed as much as they did. Eloise ate slice after slice of bread and jam and thought that she'd never seen Mo enjoy herself like this.

Even after breakfast was finished, the kitchen overflowed with noise and banter. Tommy's father unpacked his boxes of ingredients. Mo washed the dishes while Eloise and Tommy's mother dried. Tommy rocketed around the kitchen pulling out anything he thought might be useful later on.

They'd almost forgotten about Dad and Lorelei Swan. When they came in, the merriment stopped.

Dad was wearing a joke Santa hat. Lorelei Swan wore a red suit and a string of fat pearls.

Mo cleared her throat. 'Merry Christmas.'

'What's all this?' cried Dad. His voice sounded loud and false in the sudden quiet. 'A Middle Eastern feast on the birthday of Our Lord? What would the Pope say?'

Lorelei Swan tittered.

Tommy's father smiled. 'The Pope might remember that Jesus was Middle Eastern. Though not, I admit, Afghani. I hope you don't mind that we have invited ourselves for Christmas?'

'Mind?' said Dad. 'Why should I mind?' There was a pause.

'Not up to you. It's my house, not yours,' said Mo. 'And look, they're doing all the cooking.'

'Perfect Christmas, waited on hand and foot,' said Dad heartily, then realised that hadn't quite come out right. 'Not that you're servants, of course – didn't mean to suggest . . . How about a drop of bubbly?'

'Not for us, thank you,' said Tommy's mother politely. 'Our religion.'

'Oh, right – seriously? You're not allowed to? Right, okay, well. All the more for us, eh, Lorelei?

And Mo – you won't say no to a drop, will you?'

'Just a drop,' said Mo. 'Did you bring those things I asked for, Stephen?'

Dad looked blank. 'Oh, sh— Sorry. You know, it completely went out of my head. Meant to put a reminder thingy on the whatsit.'

Mo closed her eyes briefly. 'I apologise,' she said to Tommy's mother. 'Your gifts will have to wait.'

'Really, it's not necessary.' Tommy's mother patted Mo's hand. 'After all, we have no gifts for you.'

'You just being here – all this food – if that's not a gift . . .' Mo blinked fiercely.

Dad handed her a glass of champagne. 'Well, you know, Mo, if you went out and did your own flaming shopping . . . I don't see that it's my fault.'

'Excuse me!' said Tommy's father suddenly. 'Everybody out of the kitchen, please. I need room to cook. Osman and Miss Eloise, you stay and help.'

Dad clapped his hand to his head, spilling his champagne. 'Can't believe I nearly forgot! Elimination Round, here's your present, sweetheart. It's from me and Lorelei.'

'I chose it,' said Lorelei Swan.

Eloise unwrapped a bright pink leather skirt and

matching jacket. They were much too large, and anyway, they were clothes she'd never wear in a million, trillion years. If they were the last clothes on earth, she'd rather go naked than put them on. She heard a smothered laugh behind her as Tommy turned away.

Eloise smiled a tight, brief smile at Lorelei Swan, then hugged her dad. It wasn't his fault. But she did think he could have chosen something for her himself. She wondered how he had described her, that Lorelei could have thought this was the perfect present.

'Very nice,' said Dad uncertainly. Eloise had the feeling it was the first time he'd seen them, too. 'Thanks, Lorelei. Lovely.'

'You'll grow into them,' said Lorelei Swan. 'Or I could exchange them for a smaller size. We could go together, Eloise. That'd be fun, wouldn't it?'

Eloise brought out her dad's present and gave it to him, pointedly ignoring Lorelei Swan.

'What's this, El Greco? Let me guess. A book? A DVD? Or is it . . . don't tell me . . . one of your drawings?' He winked at Mo. ''Cause I need another one of those.'

Lorelei Swan laughed. 'Children's drawings are

so cute,' she said to no one in particular, and sipped her champagne.

'I think you will find Eloise is an accomplished artist,' said Tommy's mother quietly, and suddenly Eloise felt like crying. Why couldn't Dad have said something nice like that?

Dad tore off the wrapping paper and held up the picture. It was a drawing of the house – not the way it looked now, all shabby and half-drowned, but as it looked in Anna's time: fresh and alert, inhabited and inviting, windows and doors open, chairs on the terrace and the garden lush and flowering.

There was a strange silence as Dad and Lorelei Swan stared at the picture. 'That's lovely, Elbow Room,' said Dad at last. 'That's the house, is it?'

'It'll make a gorgeous memento,' said Lorelei brightly. 'When we build the new convention centre, you can hang it in your office to remind you of what used to be there.'

'*Used* to be there?' said Mo.

'You know we'll have to knock the old place down,' said Dad, his eyes still fixed on the picture.

Eloise heard someone gasp. Her heart thudded in her ears.

'Knock it *down*?' said Mo. 'What are you talking about?'

'The site is wonderful,' said Lorelei Swan coolly. 'But the building is a mess. It's not worth trying to save it. The cost of converting it would be astronomical. The plumbing alone—'

'But it's beautiful,' said Tommy. His eyes and Eloise's met across the kitchen. 'And it's so old.'

'That's exactly why it's so impractical,' explained Lorelei with a patronising smile. 'Much simpler to clear it away and start all over again.'

'Such a shame,' said Tommy's father quietly. 'Is there no value in age?'

'Apparently not,' said Mo. Her eyes flashed. 'Stephen, when I gave you the house, there was no question of *demolishing* it. You said—'

'Plans change, Mo.' Dad laid Eloise's drawing on the table. 'It's called flexibility. You have to go with the flow.'

Lorelei Swan linked her arm with Dad's. She said to Mo, 'I understand how you feel. You have an *attachment*.' She made it sound like a disease. 'But now we'll always have Eloise's lovely picture to remind us.' She raised her glass of champagne. 'Happy Christmas, everyone!'

13

The Durranis prepared a delicious meal, fragrant with spices, but Eloise barely picked at her food. She heard Dad's jokes and Lorelei's titters and Mo's sarcastic remarks as if through a fog. She stirred her dessert with a spoon and couldn't eat a mouthful. And all the time she felt as if something inside her chest were screaming and hammering to get out.

But part of her still couldn't believe that it was really going to happen: that Dad was going to knock down the house. She kept expecting him to wink at her and say, *just kidding!* It was the kind of thing Dad would do.

But he didn't.

Once he leaned across to Eloise and said in a low voice, 'That was an amazing picture you drew, El Niño. I can't believe you drew that just from memory, from that one day we went there . . .' He was thinking it out as he spoke. 'You can't have been back to the house. You couldn't have gone with Mo.' He laid down his spoon and looked at her intently. 'You haven't gone back there by yourself, have you?'

Eloise stared at her plate. Conversation around the rest of the table died away into silence, and suddenly everyone was watching her. Eloise tried to hold herself tightly, to not give anything away. But Dad knew.

'Elephant Ride, you mustn't do that. You can't go roaming around on your own. How many times have you been there? More than once?'

Lorelei Swan pressed her hand to her bosom. 'You can't let them out on their *own*,' she told Mo and the Durranis. 'It's not *safe*.'

'Rubbish,' said Mo. 'The streets aren't any more dangerous now than when I was a child.'

'How would you know?' Dad narrowed his eyes. 'When was the last time you were out on the streets? If they're dangerous enough to keep *you* inside, how much more dangerous is it for a twelve-year-old girl?'

'I can't keep her locked up, Stephen. What did you expect when you left her here? If you wanted her watched twenty-four hours a day, you should have kept her with you.'

'All I'm asking for is a little common sense, a few sensible precautions—'

Tommy's father cleared his throat. 'Perhaps we should go home now.'

Dad's hand flung out. 'Stay there, stay there. No need to ruin the party just because I'm having a discussion with my mother.'

'She isn't on the streets,' said Tommy suddenly.

Everyone's heads swung round. Eloise's eyes flicked to him, then down again.

'Osman,' murmured Tommy's mother.

'She isn't on the streets,' said Tommy again, 'if she's at the old house.'

'Well, that's even worse!' said Lorelei shrilly. 'Hanging around that old dump! There could be vagrants, rats, falling plaster. It's just irresponsible, that's what it is.'

'I'll handle this, Lorelei.'

'We really must be leaving now,' said Tommy's father firmly. He pushed back his chair and gave Mo a little bow. 'Thank you so much for allowing us to share this family day.'

Tommy's mother kissed Mo on the cheek, and then, unexpectedly, she kissed Eloise too. 'Thank you for our wonderful gift,' she said softly, smiling into Eloise's eyes. Then the Durranis left.

'Those people,' Mo pointed after them with a knife. '*Those* people know what danger is. They've been through war, bombs, refugee camps, detention centres. And you dare give them lectures about rats and falling plaster?'

'I think the real point, Mrs McCredie, is that Stephen left Eloise in your care. Allowing her to roam around without any supervision is neglect. If Child Services heard about this . . .'

Mo clenched her jaw. 'Ho-ho! Is that a *threat*, Miss Swan? Because I'm sure the National Trust would love to hear about a pristine Art Deco building that someone's planning to demolish.'

Lorelei Swan swung round to Dad. 'You told me the house wasn't covered. If it's registered by the National Trust, we can't touch it.'

'It isn't,' Dad said.

'Only because I haven't told them about it,' said Mo. 'Yet.'

'Simmer down, everybody,' soothed Dad. 'Hey, hey, this is supposed to be a celebration, isn't it? How about we leave the child-rearing to Mo, and Mo leaves the business side to us, and then we can all get along nicely.'

'She isn't my child, Stephen,' said Mo.

'But it is Stephen's house,' said Lorelei Swan sweetly. Her lips stretched in a smile, but the rest of her face didn't move at all. It was the creepiest thing Eloise had ever seen.

'Let's go into the living room and have another drink.' Dad ushered Lorelei away and a minute later there came the loud *pop* of another champagne cork.

As Mo and Eloise cleared up and washed the dishes in the kitchen, they could hear Lorelei's raised voice and Dad's quieter rumble, and then finally screams of laughter, punctuated by long stretches of silence.

'Hope they're not planning to drive back to the hotel,' said Mo. Then she added darkly, 'And I hope they're not planning to stay here.' She peeled off her rubber gloves with a weary sigh. 'Think I might have a lie down, Eloise. It's been a long day. You'll be all right?'

Eloise nodded, and hung her damp tea towel over the oven rail.

'Good girl.' Mo pottered to the door, then turned back. 'What they don't understand is that it's all about *trust*.' She looked hard at Eloise. 'You know what I'm talking about.'

Eloise nodded again, but slightly guiltily. Because as soon as Mo closed her bedroom door, she knew exactly what she was going to do.

Thunder growled overhead as Eloise eased the back door open and gingerly picked up her bicycle. Dad and Lorelei wouldn't hear her, and Mo was probably asleep by now. It was late afternoon, and the sky was slated over with dark clouds. Mo had said it wasn't going to rain. 'That thunder's just empty promises,' she'd sniffed. The air was still, close and muggy. Eloise decided not to bring a jacket. After all, she wouldn't be gone for long.

As she stood on the pedals, shifting her weight to force the bike down the street, Eloise didn't notice

Tommy peering out his front window. And when she reached the red church at the top of the hill, she didn't notice another bicycle toiling up the street behind her.

The streets were empty. Everyone was inside recovering from Christmas dinner, and the town was deserted. The shops were shut, no cars were on the road, and the lowering sky brooded over the paddocks. Eloise hurried on, anxious to escape from the eerie atmosphere, anxious to slip across into Anna's time. Anna's house could never be demolished; Anna's garden was safe.

Eloise let the bike drop near the front steps and began to run. She wanted to hurtle through into the other time, right through that invisible wall, through the muffling barrier of silence, and burst out into Anna's protected, sunlit world.

She closed her eyes as she ran. The noises of her own time fell away like the dry husk of a cicada, and the wave dumped her on the shore of the other time, soft and vulnerable. Eloise opened her eyes.

And saw a different world.

Eloise felt jarred, as if something had struck her on the side of the head. This was all wrong. This was

a nightmare. It couldn't be. She closed her eyes and
flicked them open again.

There was no house. No swimming pool. No
summerhouse. They were gone.

The pitiless sun beat down on a wasteland. There
were trees and a bald stretch of earth where the lawn
should be, but there was nothing like a garden – just a
half-dead tangle of plants, fallen branches, uprooted
bushes, and weeds. Where the pool should have been,
there was a kind of sunken place strewn with rubble
and broken bricks. Where the summerhouse had
stood, Eloise saw shards of splintered white timber,
gleaming pale against raw dirt.

She stumbled up the slope toward the place where
the house should have been. But there was only a
blasted landscape of dust and rubble, smashed concrete
and broken tiles, twisted iron and shattered glass.

'Anna? Anna!' she called out, her voice weak and
shrill in the stillness.

From a branch above her, an unseen magpie
cawed. Eloise jumped in fright, bashing her ankle on
a jagged chunk of concrete. The magpie eyed her
sideways, then spread its wings and silently swooped
down at her.

Eloise cried out, covering her head with her arms, and stumbled away, sliding and scrabbling across the rubble. The magpie's wings grazed her hair, and she beat the air with her hands. 'Anna!' she screamed. 'Anna!'

The magpie swooped again, and this time its beak struck Eloise's head. She threw herself forward, away from the wasteland of rocks and dust, across the mangy stretch of ground where the lawn had been, crashing between the thick stalks of thistles and dandelions that snatched at her bare legs.

She was still crying for Anna, though she knew Anna was gone. In this place, there was no Anna. She sobbed for breath. The garden had turned against her: smashed walls and swooping birds, thorns and prickles. *Let me go home. I want to go home!*

But this time the garden didn't want to let her go. Eloise stumbled forward and back, trying to beat her way back to her own time. She called for Anna, but she was alone in this wild time, this bleak and barren time, and there was no way out.

Eloise screamed and screamed. The noise filled her ears, blotting out everything. She screamed until the world went black.

14

Eloise woke into night.

She lay on her back in the long grass, staring up into the dark. A hard lump of pain pressed into the middle of her back. Slowly she sat up.

The sun had set while she was in the other time. Clouds blanketed the sky; there was no moon, no stars, just blackness overhead. A growl of thunder shook the ground, and Eloise clambered up. Her hands were trembling. She didn't understand. Where had it all gone? Where was Anna? Where was the summerhouse and the main house and the pool?

A horrible thought struck her: what if she was still trapped there, in the ruined time? She whirled around. Her eyes had started to adjust to the dark and she could just make out the pale shape of the summerhouse behind her, shrouded in its cape of ivy, and the ghostly scaffolding of the diving board looming out of the dark.

Eloise groped toward the summerhouse, and even before she reached it she knew that she was back in her own time. The summerhouse was overgrown, the curtain of ivy hung over the door. When she touched the archway, she felt splinters, not the smooth painted wood of Anna's time. But what could have *happened* to Anna's time? Where had it gone?

The first drops of rain spattered onto the leaves, and then on Eloise's head. She hesitated; should she run for her bike and race home to Mo's, or shelter in the summerhouse until the rain stopped? It must be late; even Mo would have noticed by now that she wasn't home . . . But on the other hand, she didn't want to ride through a rainstorm . . .

Then she heard a faint sound, so faint that she wasn't sure if she'd imagined it. A human sound, coming from the swimming pool. She tiptoed to the edge. Rain was falling faster now, splattering the concrete until it blurred to a grey slickness. Eloise peered over the edge of the pool, and at that moment lightning crackled overhead and lit up the garden with a strobe-light flash.

A body was lying at the bottom of the swimming pool.

Eloise knelt on the wet concrete, her heart thudding hard. Her lips shaped the word, *Tommy?*

As if he'd heard her, he groaned and lifted his head, then let it fall back onto the mat of dead leaves.

He must have fallen in. He was hurt. She could never get him out on her own. She would have to get help. Her heart squeezed up small with fear. She couldn't do this. She didn't know what to do.

Lightning flashed again, and Eloise stood up. At the junction where the red church stood was a small blue sign: TURNER–BUNGAREE DISTRICT HOSPITAL. All she'd have to do was stick to the road and keep on riding until she ran into it.

It was really raining now. Eloise was so wet already that it was pointless to worry about getting any wetter. Her hair clung to her head, rain poured down her eyebrows and into her mouth. She ran through the wet grass, swish, swish, toward the house, back to where she'd dropped her bike, a dark knot of metal on the gravel. A second dark knot lay nearby: Tommy's bike. What was he doing here? Had he followed her? Or come to find her? Had Mo sent him to look for her? Or . . .

There wasn't time to think about it now. Eloise lifted up her bike; the handlebars were slippery, the wheels skidded on the wet gravel. As she pushed off she nearly slipped sideways. But then she had it; she just had to hold on tight, and focus, and pedal tight and careful. Under the pine trees, the ground was almost dry, but it was so dark she almost crashed into the trees.

Out on the road, the tarmac was slick and the rain came down in curtains. Eloise could just make out the white posts that marked the edge of the road. She swung the bike to the right, away from the town, the direction she'd never been. The bike skidded under her but she managed to steady it. Squinting into the rain, Eloise steered from one white post to the next. If a car came zooming along in the wet, it would never see her in time to stop. The dress she'd worn in honour of Christmas dinner clung to her legs. She began to shiver. She'd almost forgotten where she was supposed to be riding to; she seemed to have been pushing the bike onward forever into the dark, into the rain.

Suddenly the bike slewed from under her. Eloise hurtled sideways, the bike smashed down on her; pain gashed across her leg, and her hands scraped gravel. She'd come off at the side of the road. She wasn't badly hurt, but her whole body was trembling as she stood up and groped to heave the bike upright. Her hands hurt. Something was wrong with the bike; the bike wouldn't stand, it wouldn't go. The chain dangled loose from the gears, and one wheel was bent.

Eloise flung the bike away; she'd just have to go on foot. But the accident had muddled her. She wasn't sure which direction she'd come from and which way she was going. The dark was thick all around her; the rain drove down onto the top of her head. She was almost sure she had to go this way. She bent her head into the rain and tried to run, but the rain pushed against her like a hand to her chest.

It was almost like wading through water, almost like swimming. *Keep swimming through.* She thought about Tommy at the bottom of the pool. If it kept on raining, the pool would fill with water; he might drown. She thought of Mo, of Dad and Lorelei. She thought about Anna. She had the strangest feeling that she was walking away from Anna, that every step carried her further away. But she had to help Tommy, he was the one who needed her now.

Eloise put one foot in front of the other, one, two, one, two, jogging, walking, jogging again. A numb, dizzy chant circled through her head: *keep on swimming, keep on swimming.* The road dipped and rose beneath her feet, and then at last, very far away, lights twinkled out of the dark, and very slowly, with every dip in the road, the lights grew brighter and bigger until at last Eloise staggered into a world of light, a world that was dry and hot and dazzlingly bright.

She stood in front of the hospital desk, dripping and shaking. A nurse looked up.

'Hey there, sweetie. Wow, look at you. You're soaked! What's the matter, what's happened?'

Eloise opened her mouth. For a dreadful moment she thought nothing would happen, but then she heard her own voice, faint and far away, even though she felt as if she were shouting.

'*Help.*'

The ambulance careered through the night, lights flashing, siren wailing, windscreen wipers slashing back and forth. Eloise sat in the back, wrapped in a blanket. She shivered so violently that her teeth clashed together. Someone had given her a plastic cup of hot chocolate to drink, but she'd spilled most of it.

The journey that had taken Eloise so long by foot lasted only a few minutes in the ambulance. In fact, they drove past the house in the dark and had to turn back.

But when they'd bumped down the pine-tree tunnel and wailed to a halt, there was a car already parked on the gravel in front of the house: a big blue four-wheel drive.

'Which way, love? Where is he?'

Eloise's arms and legs were stiff and heavy but she managed to clamber out of the ambulance and stagger across the grass. Someone pulled out a fat torch and a beam of light swept across the face of the house. The rain had almost stopped. The drops sparkled in the light like a fall of tinsel.

Around the corner of the house Eloise saw another, thinner beam of light, swinging drunkenly back and forth; a faint glow shone from behind the wide back windows. Voices called her name. They were looking in the wrong places; they were nowhere near the summerhouse. Didn't Dad know she'd be at the summerhouse?

But that was Anna's dad, not hers . . . and anyway, she *wasn't* there . . .

Eloise stumbled headlong down the slope, calling, 'This way, here, he's down here!'

The white shaft of torchlight jerked across the summerhouse and lit up the diving board. Eloise flung herself down on her stomach at the edge of the pool. 'There, there he is, there.'

And then everything became a blur of shouts and light and flurried movement, lowered stretchers and radio calls. And suddenly Dad was there, white in the torchlight, grabbing her into his arms, pressing her against his black parka all slick with rain. And Lorelei Swan was behind him, wearing a battered old raincoat that must have been Mo's, her hair flattened to her skull. Someone yelled at her to please hold the torch steady. Dad was asking a million questions, half-shaking her and half-hugging her, not waiting for her to answer, and someone asked if he knew the parents and someone else said *Wait a sec, I think it's Najela Durrani's boy*.

And then someone else was asking Dad questions, and the torch was shining in their eyes, and Dad held Eloise away from the light, and he kept saying, *I just want to take her home. I just want to take her home.* And his voice was getting louder and louder. And Lorelei Swan's voice was shrill in the background and then Dad yelled at her, and she yelled back, and Dad gripped Eloise tighter and tighter, and she craned around his arm to watch as they winched Tommy out of the pool, strapped onto a stretcher under a silver blanket with his eyes shut, and she wriggled away from Dad and Lorelei Swan and ran over to the ambulance man who had his hand on Tommy and was saying, *You're going to be all right, mate. It's all right now.* And he saw Eloise and winked at her and said, *Don't worry, love. He's broken his arm but he's going to be okay.*

And then Dad grabbed her again and marched her up the slope, and Lorelei Swan tripped and swayed behind them, all wet and bedraggled and saying, *You need to focus on what's important here, Stephen.*

And Dad swung round and yelled at her, 'My daughter is what's important here, Lorelei!'

And Lorelei yelled, 'Well, if that's the way you feel, you can shove it!'

And Dad yelled, 'Fine, I will!' And then he swung Eloise around again and kept marching her up the hill through the wet grass. Lorelei Swan yelled after them, 'I suppose you're going to leave me here now, are you? In the rain? In the dark, in the middle of nowhere?'

'Get in the car!' Dad hollered at her, and he pushed Eloise up into the front seat and buckled her in as if she was still a little kid and kissed her on the head, and Lorelei Swan scrambled into the back seat, sniffing. Dad got in and turned up the heater full bore and they bumped down the driveway behind the ambulance. But at the end of the driveway the ambulance roared away to the right and Dad swung the four-wheel drive to the left, toward home.

15

'T ommy followed you to the house yesterday afternoon. But after you got there, he lost you somehow.' Mo lowered herself onto the end of Eloise's bed. 'And then it got dark so suddenly, with the storm coming. I suppose he must have been looking for you when he tumbled into the pool. It was very naughty, Eloise, to sneak off like that. Especially after what everyone had been saying. You gave us all such a fright.'

Eloise whispered, 'I'm sorry.'

'Well,' said Mo as she lifted a strand of Eloise's hair back from her forehead, 'I suppose it was worth it, if it's brought you back into the land of the living. I mean the land of the speaking. Mind you, I'm not sure Tommy will see it like that, nor his parents.'

'Is he okay?' said Eloise huskily.

'Broken arm, mild hypothermia, and a bruised behind,' said Mo. 'They kept him at the hospital last night but he'll be home this morning. Might be worth you going next door later with a big bunch of flowers and an apology.'

Eloise squirmed. 'Not flowers.'

'For his mother, not for Tommy!' Mo smiled, and patted Eloise's leg under the blanket. 'How are you feeling, anyway, chicken, after that big sleep?'

'Good.'

'Well, you can stay there for the moment. Dr Durrani says a day in bed won't hurt you. I'm going to make some sandwiches.'

Eloise thought about protesting, but then she snuggled down. It really was nice to be tucked up in bed. She felt so heavy and limp, as if she'd never move again . . . Before too long she was asleep.

At lunchtime Dad arrived. 'Well, that's that,' he announced, with an odd mixture of gloom and triumph. 'She's gone. Stormed off back to Melbourne.'

'Who has? You mean Lorelei Swan?' exclaimed Mo. 'I thought we were going to be stuck with her forever.'

Eloise wriggled with satisfaction. Then she remembered she could speak if she wanted to, and she whispered, 'Good.'

Dad threw her a startled glance. 'My God. So it's true. You're talking again—'

'She's a human, Stephen, not a hamster,' said Mo brusquely. 'No need to treat her like a sideshow freak just because she can talk.'

'Well, no, but . . .' Dad bent down and kissed Eloise on the forehead. 'It's good to have you back, Elocution Lessons.'

'Um, Dad,' said Eloise shyly. 'Would it be okay if you just called me my name?'

Dad's eyebrows shot upward. 'Yeah, sure,' he said after a minute. 'I guess so. I thought you liked all my funny little nicknames.'

'I like Eloise better,' said Eloise firmly.

Mo plumped down on the bed. 'I want to hear more about Lorelei Swan.'

'Nothing more to tell.' Dad shrugged. 'She's gone, vamoosed, cleared out, skedaddled. We had a bit of a row last night, while we were out searching for this young lady. What was all that about, by the way?'

'I just wanted to go for a ride,' said Eloise. 'I'm sorry everyone was so worried.'

'Yes, well. So we bloody well were. All hell broke loose once we realised you were gone, and of course the storm had started by then and it was pitch dark. Were you sheltering in the house, or what?'

'Mm,' said Eloise uncomfortably. 'It was raining.'

'And then young Tommy had his fall and you rushed off for help? I don't know whether to be proud of you for that, or angry with you for taking off in the first place. Anyway, tempers were running quite high as you can imagine. Lorelei and I had words, and the upshot is, she's gone.' He ran his hand through his hair. 'I've got a lot of sweet-talking to do. Thought I might start work on an email, so it'll be waiting when she gets back to Melbourne.'

Eloise and Mo exchanged a look. 'You're better off without her, if you ask me,' said Mo. 'Which I know you weren't.'

'No, I wasn't. But it's the money, Mo, I need her money. Simple as that.'

Mo stood up. 'Come on, Eloise. Get dressed. While your father starts on his sweet-talking, you and I are going to pay a visit next door.'

Dad and Eloise gaped.

'But Mo,' said Dad, 'you haven't set foot out of this house for I don't know how many years . . .'

'And I think it's time that changed, don't you?' said Mo crossly. 'If Eloise can bring herself to talk again, I'm sure I can go for a little walk.'

Mo was very brave. It took her quite a while to get ready; she had to arm herself with a hat and dark glasses and an umbrella to clutch in one hand while she held onto Eloise's arm with the other. Then she stood in the doorway for a minute or two, breathing deeply.

'Come on, Maureen Jean,' she muttered to herself. 'You can do it. Here we go. One step – there. No, no, not yet. Just a minute.' She lurched back inside. 'Just a minute.'

'I'm with you, Mo,' said Eloise. 'I won't let anything happen to you.' Eloise was holding in her other hand the flowers that Dad had bought for Tommy's mother.

'How far do you reckon it is to next door?' said
Mo. 'Twenty steps?'

'Maybe only fifteen,' Eloise assured her. She
squeezed Mo's hand. 'We can make it.'

Mo breathed again, wedged her dark glasses on
her nose, and launched herself out of the house,
counting firmly, 'One, two, three, four . . .'

It took them forty-nine steps to reach the Durranis'
front door. Mo leaned against the wall, breathing
hard, while Eloise rang the doorbell.

'That wasn't too bad,' said Mo, reaching up to
touch her hat with a shaking hand. 'Don't know what
all the fuss was about.'

Tommy's father answered the door. It was hard
to say whether he was more surprised to see Mo
standing on the step, or to hear Eloise say, 'These
are for you, and I'm very sorry about Tommy.'

'Remember I told you if I wanted help, I'd ask for
it?' Mo said to him as they stepped inside. 'Consider
yourself asked.'

Tommy's mother was at work but Tommy's father
led them into the living room and offered them a
cup of tea. Tommy was lying on the couch with his
eyes closed and his arm in plaster. He struggled up

at the sight of Eloise and her grandmother.

'Stay there, Tommy, we won't disturb you.' Mo waved him down again. 'I'd just as soon have my tea in the kitchen, if you don't mind, Professor. I'm a little nervous, to tell you the truth, being inside someone else's house.'

'We're honoured you chose our house to visit.' Tommy's dad made his little bow. 'Tommy and I were about to start a game of chess; perhaps Eloise would take my place?'

Eloise sat down hesitantly on the other side of a small table where a chessboard was set up, and eyed it with some trepidation. The adults moved down the hallway to the kitchen, still talking.

Tommy and Eloise sat in silence. The Durranis' house was very neat, with not much furniture. A clock ticked slowly on the mantel above the gas heater. Eloise's portrait of Tommy was propped beside it. Eloise hastily looked away.

At last Tommy said, 'So you're talking now?'

Eloise nodded.

'You know how to play chess?'

'No.'

There was a pause.

'Thanks for last night,' said Tommy awkwardly. 'Getting the ambulance and that.'

'Sorry I made you fall in the pool,' said Eloise.

'You didn't make me. I just didn't see it. Should watch where I'm going, eh.'

There was another pause. Eloise picked up a chess piece and twiddled it in her fingers.

'So,' said Tommy. 'Where did you go?'

Eloise dropped the chess piece abruptly and bent down to pick it up. 'Um – I went to the house.'

'I know that; I was following you, remember? I mean after that. You ran across the grass and you just . . . disappeared. Into the air. Like that.' Tommy clicked his fingers.

'Um,' said Eloise, going pink. She remembered that this was the trouble with talking: people expected you to answer questions you didn't want to answer.

'I was watching you,' said Tommy. 'I know what I saw. So don't make out you went in the little – what's-it-called? That little round house. Or inside the big house. It wasn't dark then, I saw you. You just went invisible.' Tommy was scowling at her, but not, Eloise realised, in an angry way. He just really wanted to know.

Without meaning to, Eloise heard herself say, 'You won't believe me.'

'I might. If I promise to believe, will you tell me?'

'You can't promise to believe.'

'I'll try. Come on, if you can't tell me, who can you tell?'

'Okay,' said Eloise after a minute. 'This is what happened. I don't know how, but I think I went back in time.' She shot a look at Tommy, but his face was still, listening politely. 'I went back into the past to when the house was new, and I made friends with a girl called Anna. And . . .' She took a deep breath. 'Anna was my mother, when she was a little girl. She died two years ago,' whispered Eloise. 'But in the house, she was alive. We were friends. We did stuff together. She was a little girl.'

For a moment Tommy didn't say anything. Then he said carefully, 'Are you sure the little girl was your mum, Eloise? Because Mo is your dad's mother, right? And it was Mo's house. *Her* family lived there.'

Eloise stared at the chessboard.

'It was your dad who grew up in Turner, wasn't it? But he didn't live in the big house either. He lived next door, here, with Mo.'

'But Anna,' faltered Eloise. 'I met her. She was a little girl. I went into her time.' But even as she spoke, she knew that Tommy was right. Her other grandparents had come from Hobart. Mum was from Hobart. Not Turner. Her throat thickened so that she could hardly swallow. She choked out, 'You must think I'm so dumb.'

'Hey,' said Tommy. 'You think that's dumb, you should try falling into an empty swimming pool.'

'But . . . she *was* called Anna. And I *did* go back in time, I must have. The house was all different and there were people living there. And the garden . . . We painted pictures in the summerhouse, and the pool was full of water, we swam in it. I saw it; I did, lots of times!' Eloise angrily dashed tears from her cheeks.

'Maybe it was a different Anna,' suggested Tommy. 'Not your mum, another Anna. Was there someone called Anna in Mo's family maybe?'

'But she *looked* like me!' insisted Eloise. 'I always looked like Mum, the only bit of me that looks like Dad's family is my stupid hair! And then when I went to find her yesterday, it was all different. It was all gone. The house was gone. Everything was ruined . . . Maybe I'll never find her again . . .'

Tommy's eyes widened, and he sat bolt upright. 'I got it.'

'Got what?'

'You got a pen? I'll show you. Never mind, there's one here somewhere.' Tommy scrabbled around under the coffee table with his good arm and surfaced with a pen and the back of an envelope. 'Look, look. You say you went into the past, right?'

'Right . . .'

'Okay, well, just suppose you did travel in time, but you went the *other way*? What if you didn't go back? What if you went *forward*?' Tommy drew emphatic arrows on the envelope.

Eloise stared. 'You mean . . . into the future?'

'Yeah, into the future.'

'But the house was all new. There were builders there and fresh paint, and the garden was all neat and tidy . . .'

'Were the plants small or fully grown?'

'Well . . . they were tall.'

'The builders, the painters and that, they were fixing the place up!' said Tommy excitedly. 'Not building it, they were fixing it up again, see? But when you went yesterday to find her, this Anna girl and everything was all gone?'

Eloise nodded.

Tommy tapped the envelope. 'So what happened yesterday to *change the future*?'

'Dad,' whispered Eloise. 'Dad and Lorelei. They're going to knock the house down.'

'So when you went into the future last night, you went into a *different* future,' said Tommy triumphantly. He scribbled wildly on the envelope and thrust it at Eloise. All she could see were arrows, looped and branching, tangled ribbons. 'It's an alternative reality, see?'

Eloise looked at him blankly.

'Okay,' said Tommy patiently. 'Maybe it's like this. Maybe time is like a piece of string. But instead of being in a straight line, the string's got looped; it's crossing over itself. So when you travel in time, it's the place where the string crosses itself, get it? Where the two points on the string touch.'

'Ye-es,' said Eloise uncertainly.

'So yesterday, it was like the string frayed into two threads. What was the plan before your dad decided to knock the house down?'

'We were going to live there. He was going to turn it into a hotel or something.'

'Well, that's one thread. Down that thread the house is a hotel or whatever. You live there and sometime Anna gets born, so she's there when you meet her in the future. But down the *other* thread there's no house, no hotel and you move away. There's no Anna – she never gets born. You get it?'

'Um,' said Eloise, feeling slightly dizzy. 'But then – if Anna's not my mum . . .' She swallowed. 'If she's in the future, who is she? Do you think she might be . . . She might be my daughter.'

Tommy sucked in his breath. 'Wow. *Freaky.*'

'So, that would mean Anna's father was my . . .' Eloise went pink and changed the subject. 'So you *do* believe that I switched times?'

'I'm not saying I *believe* it.' Tommy frowned. 'It's just a hypothesis, right? A theory. It might be true, it might not. But, you know, scientists talk about time travel and wormholes, cuts in the fabric of the universe, alternative worlds, stuff like that. Hey,' he looked up at her suddenly. 'Did you ever see Anna's mum? Did you see if she was you?'

'No. She was away. Anna was really missing her.'

'Well, she got to see you anyway, didn't she? That's freaky. It's as if she was calling you and you came.'

But Eloise was thinking about something else. 'But what's *happened* to Anna? Where's she gone?'

Tommy shrugged. 'Gone. Unless you can get the alternative reality back.'

'But how can I do that?'

Tommy looked at her as if she were an idiot. 'That's easy. You've just got to stop your dad knocking the house down.'

Eloise stared at him for a minute, and then she jumped up. The chessboard crashed to the ground and Tommy started to pick up the pieces.

'Don't worry about that!' cried Eloise. 'Quick! We have to talk to Mo.'

16

They found Dad in the dining room, gloomily typing an apology to Lorelei Swan on his laptop.

'Never been any good at grovelling,' he said without looking up. 'You're a writer, Mo, want to give me a hand?'

'I have better uses for my talents,' said Mo. She pulled out a chair across the table, sat down and folded her hands in front of her. Eloise sat down beside Dad. They both stared at him intently until he looked up.

'Hello!' He gave an uneasy laugh. 'What's all this?'

'A business proposal,' said Eloise.

Dad laughed and ruffled her hair. 'Taking after the old man, are you? I hope you have better luck than I've had.'

'We're serious, Stephen,' said Mo crossly. 'Be quiet for once in your life and listen.' She looked at Eloise. 'Go on.'

Eloise took a deep breath. 'Dad.'

'Yes, Ella Fitz— Yes, Eloise?'

'You don't *have* to knock down the house, do you?'

'I meant what I said about the National Trust,' warned Mo. 'You demolish that house over my dead body.'

'Won't have to wait long then, will I?'

'Very amusing.'

'But come on, what else can I do with the place? I can't convert it to a hotel, it'd cost a fortune. And Lorelei won't fund it. She wants something new.'

'Let's put Lorelei to one side for the moment,' said Mo. 'Eloise has an idea.'

Eloise knew she had to get this right. Their whole lives, Anna's very existence, depended on it. She clasped her hands together and tried to keep her voice steady. 'I heard about this artist place. Where artists and writers and musicians can go to stay and work.'

Dad looked startled. 'You mean an artists' retreat.'

'Where *did* you hear about that, Eloise?' asked Mo, with genuine curiosity.

'Um, on TV. But I thought . . . couldn't you make the house into one of those?'

Dad rubbed his chin. 'I don't know . . .'

'Artists might not mind things being a bit rough around the edges,' put in Mo. 'Sharing bathrooms and so on.'

'As long as it was peaceful, and they could get on with their work,' said Eloise.

'Plenty of room, decent food,' said Mo. 'They'd like a bit of character to the place, all the old fittings. Adds to the charm.'

'It's not such a bad idea,' admitted Dad. 'Wouldn't be able to charge as much money, mind you, but the overheads would be lower . . .' Then he shook his head regretfully. 'Lorelei would never go for it.'

'Is money all you ever think about?' said Mo.

'No,' said Dad. 'But I do *have* to think about it. I've got a daughter to provide for, you know.'

'I'm okay, Dad,' said Eloise. 'As long as I've got pencils and paper and paint, I'm happy. And a pool,' she added.

'If it would help,' said Mo, 'I could sell this place.'

Dad stared. 'Are you serious? But where would you live?'

'She'd move in with us, of course,' said Eloise happily. 'In the big house.'

'Don't look at me like that,' said Mo. 'You'll need help running the place if this scheme's going to work, and you won't have to pay me. *And* I'm a writer. Aren't you going to have writers there? Maybe a change of scene is just what I need to get my damn book finished. I'm sick to death of it, to tell you the truth. And you can't organise your way out of a paper bag, you'll need me. You can do the talking part, that's what you're good at, and I can run the office, do the accounts and so on. Like I used to do for your father. Wouldn't mind doing that again.'

'Mo . . . I don't know what to say.'

'Just say you'll do it. I dare say I can even find you some clients. Lots of my friends are artists and writers and that sort.'

'But Mo,' said Eloise hesitantly, 'I didn't think you . . .'

'You didn't think I had any friends?' Mo sniffed. 'What an old-fashioned child you are. I've got hundred of friends *online*. Ever heard of blogs and chat rooms? You don't think I spend all day slaving away at *A Brief History of Sea Voyages*, do you? A girl's got to have some fun.'

'Blow me down,' said Dad blankly, then he jumped up and began to pace. 'Basic structure's pretty sound, just a few repairs – painting, obviously – maybe six rooms upstairs? Self-contained cabins in the grounds. All eco-friendly of course. Have to look into digging for bore water.' He stopped suddenly and shook his head. 'You really think we can do this?'

'I know we can,' cried Eloise. She snatched up the picture of the house she'd drawn for Dad and pushed it toward him. 'Look! See how lovely it can be.'

Dad took the drawing and stared at it. 'Yes,' he whispered. 'Maybe you're right . . .' A dreamy look came over his face, a look that Eloise had seen many times before, as if he were peering into the future, as if he could see the writers and musicians and artists moving across the terrace, waving at him from the windows.

'No one has conventions any more,' said Mo. Eloise thought she looked crafty. 'That's all old hat. It's all videoconferencing these days. No, no, you need to focus on the creative industries. They always do well when the economy gets a bit shaky.'

'Hm,' said Dad. 'I guess so . . .'

Suddenly his phone began to buzz, and they all jumped. Dad flipped it open.

'Ah, Lorelei,' he said. 'I was going to call you.'

Eloise and Mo looked at each other. The insect whine of Lorelei's voice hummed from the phone.

'Yes,' said Dad. 'Yes, but . . . the thing is, Lorelei, there's been a change of plan. Mo and Eloise have come up with a new scheme – an artists' retreat.'

There was an explosion at the other end of the phone.

'Really?' said Dad. 'I thought it was a pretty good idea, myself . . . Oh? You need to be flexible, Lorelei. Go with the flow . . . Mm, it's a shame you feel like that. But actually, I don't think we're going to need your money after all . . .' He winked at Eloise and Mo and kept talking. 'Have to run the figures, but factoring out the projected construction costs . . .'

Mo stood up and laid a hand on Eloise's shoulder. 'Come on,' she said. 'Let's leave him to it. You can give me a hand with dinner.'

17

It was a couple of weeks before Mo felt ready to walk to the big house, with Tommy on one side and Eloise on the other. Dad was going to pick them up later, so they only had to walk one way.

Eloise had been back to the house with Dad, helping him to measure and take photos and make plans. But she hadn't been there alone, so there'd been no chance to try to slip through into the other time. Eloise wondered if she could go through, even if she tried, and wondered what would be waiting if she did.

They walked very slowly through the empty back streets. Mo couldn't face the main road yet. But Tommy's father said it probably wouldn't be long.

Three times a week he and Mo sat out in the garden and talked about things. 'Clever man, your father,' Mo told Tommy. 'I always said so.' And Eloise had started talking to him too, once a week, and even Dad had said he'd think about it.

But today none of them talked much as they walked along through the summer morning, under the high blue sky.

At last they arrived at the sagging gates and the tunnel of pines. When the house came into view, Mo stopped in the middle of the driveway and peered ahead, fanning herself with her battered straw hat.

'Gloomy old pile, isn't it,' she said. 'I'd forgotten how depressing it is. No wonder I ran away from it. Maybe this artists' colony-retreat-whatsit isn't such a good idea after all.'

'No!' cried Eloise. 'It's not depressing! It looks sad now, but when it's fixed up, and the garden's full of flowers, and those big windows are all clean, it's lovely. It *will* be lovely, I mean,' she corrected herself hastily. 'You'll see.' She adjusted her sunhat and said softly, 'I just wish Mum could see it. She would have loved it here.'

Mo glanced down at Eloise. 'She did see it, you

know. She came here with your father, years ago, before you were born. She said it was a beautiful old house.' Mo squeezed Eloise's shoulder. 'You're right, she would have loved it.'

Eloise put her hand on Mo's and they stood in silence for a moment. It was funny, Eloise thought. She'd been afraid of talking about Mum, of even thinking about her. But now she realised that not thinking about her had hurt more than remembering ever could.

Eloise smiled. 'Wait till we paint it,' she said. 'It'll be splendiferous.'

Mo raised an eyebrow. 'I must say, if you weren't so sure of yourself, I'd be tempted to give up now.'

'Giving up and running away isn't our family failing any more, remember?' said Eloise.

'I suppose the new family failing is going to be the pursuit of foolish dreams,' said Mo. 'Though, come to think of it, there's been some of that in the past, too.'

'Come on,' said Eloise firmly. 'Come on, Tommy. I want to show you properly in the daylight.'

As she steered them both round the biggest holes in the driveway, she thought, *It's because of Anna that I'm so sure. If she hadn't shown me how beautiful this house could be, maybe I'd feel like giving up too*. And she felt a wave of gratitude toward her summerhouse girl.

Maybe it would be Eloise's job now to stop Mo and Dad from giving up. She knew that running away was a hard habit to break, and they had both been doing it for a lot longer than she had. Well, she'd help them, and Tommy's dad would help too. All the Durranis would help, just by being around; they were the kind of people who never gave up. Eloise hoped some of that would rub off on the McCredies.

At the front steps, Mo stopped again and stared up at the house. Then she turned slowly around, took off her dark glasses, and gazed out at the garden. She breathed out a great big sigh.

'There's a terrible amount of work here,' she complained. 'I'm too old to start something like this.'

'But I'm not.' Tommy squeezed her arm. 'Neither is Eloise. We'll do all the work, won't we, El? You just sit in a chair and order us around. You're good at that.'

He winked at Eloise, and Eloise smiled back. Tommy was helping already.

'We-ell,' said Mo. 'I suppose so.'

She cheered up slightly when they showed her the back of the house. 'I thought all these shrubs would have died. But they just need a good prune. Oh, this is more like it. I suppose it is quite a pretty house. Underneath. It's just so damn big.'

'It's too big for one person,' said Eloise. 'It wants to be full of people.'

Mo squinted into the distance. 'Is that . . . Where's the summerhouse gone?'

'Over here.' Tommy pointed. 'Next to the pool. The pool where I had my accident.'

'Have to put a fence around that too, I suppose,' grumbled Mo. 'More expense. All right, lead on. Let's see if it's as bad as I remember.'

Eloise hung back while Tommy and Mo picked their way through the long grass. It would be awful if she accidentally slipped into the other time while Mo and Tommy were there. She was sure now that if she did go through it would be Anna's time again, not the horrible alternative time when the house was gone and everything was ruined. Eloise was sure *that* time would never come true now.

She would have liked to see Anna again; she

missed her. Except, if she and Tommy were right and Anna was her daughter, of course she would see her again . . . But that would be different. Eloise had a feeling that the time to be Anna's friend was over and the time to be Anna's mother wasn't here yet. And that one summer, years and years and years from now, Anna would meet her own summerhouse girl, and not find out her name until the very end . . .

Suddenly it struck Eloise that Anna must have known who she really was. When she found out Eloise's name. Eloise wasn't such a common name. She must have guessed, thought Eloise, or she would have said, *Hey, that's my mumma's name* . . . At the very end, she *must* have known.

Then it really wouldn't be right to see Anna now, with both of them knowing who they truly were, not even to say goodbye. Eloise's goodbye would have to be the painting in the summerhouse, where the two girls held out their hands to one another across the garden, through the water, across the silence and the stream of time. The summerhouse girls.

So Eloise didn't walk over the grass with Mo and Tommy. Instead, she turned and made her way along the back terrace to the open door and slipped inside the big house.

Last time she was here she'd felt uneasy, as if she didn't belong. Not today. Sun streamed through the windows, dust motes danced in the air. The house was coming to life today; it knew it was wanted, it was preparing itself to be reborn. The house gathered Eloise in and embraced her, and she realised she was smiling.

She ran up the curving stairs and along each of the corridors, flinging open the door to every room to let the sunshine pierce to the very heart of the house. The big windows blazed with light, and Eloise danced back to the curved window of the gallery and laughed, breathless, as she pressed her hands against the glass and peered down across the lawn to the quivering trees and the tip of the summerhouse roof. She banged on the window and shouted, and after a moment Tommy appeared and waved. He cupped his hands to his mouth and called something Eloise couldn't hear, but she shouted back, 'I'm coming!'

She skimmed the tips of her fingers along the curve of the railing as she ran down the stairs, holding on to her hat with her other hand.

And saw a flicker of movement at the bottom of the stairs.

The back of Eloise's neck went cold. She saw a girl in shorts and a blue T-shirt at the foot of the steps, gazing up wide-eyed with terror, gazing at *her*. Stiffly, rigid with fear, the girl stepped back into the shadows of the foyer.

Eloise reached the bottom of the stairs. She held herself still, not wanting to frighten her more, and then slowly, carefully, she turned her head and looked straight at the other girl.

Their eyes met. The girl in the blue top backed away, one step, then another. And suddenly the foyer was empty. The girl was gone.

Eloise stood still for a moment, her heart beating fast, looking at the place where the other girl, her younger self, had been.

Then she walked out of the foyer, out of the back door, out into the summer day.

Tommy came running up to meet her. 'Hey, Mo wants to fill in the swimming pool! She can't do that, it's cool! Dangerous, hey, but cool.'

'I won't let her,' said Eloise. 'I love swimming. When we live here, I'm going to swim every day.'

'You good at swimming?' Tommy fell into step beside her. 'You better get on the team at school; we need good swimmers. And did I tell you about the school paper? It's online now. Mrs Mithen runs it. She'll want you to put pictures in, I bet, cartoons and that. Man, she's going to *love* you.'

Eloise had almost forgotten that school was starting in a couple of weeks. She wondered if she would be good enough for the swimming team. At her other schools, she'd always been too scared to try out.

'Put solar panels on the roof,' Tommy was saying. 'Water tanks, a wind turbine even. Man, you're lucky! I *love* this place. There's *heaps* of stuff we could do here.' He stopped. 'Heaps of stuff *you* could do, I mean,' he said awkwardly. 'If you want to. I don't want to take over, you know?'

'I know,' said Eloise. 'That's okay.'

Abruptly Tommy stopped, and scowled down at the grass. 'Hey, Eloise.'

'Yeah?'

'Can you do me a favour? Can you draw me a picture?'

'Sure. What of?'

'You?'

'Okay,' she said after a minute. 'I guess so.'

'Cool.' Tommy scowled off into the distance, and without looking at Eloise he stuck out his strong brown hand. Eloise frowned but took it, and they ran like little kids toward the summerhouse, with the earth solid beneath their feet, the sun in their hair, and behind them the big white house where the rest of their lives were waiting.

about
the author

Kate Constable was born in Melbourne. She spent some of her childhood in Papua New Guinea, without television but close to a library where she 'inhaled' stories. She studied Law at uni before realising this was a mistake, then worked in a record company when it was still fun. She left the music industry to write the Chanters of Tremaris series: *The Singer of All Songs, The Waterless Sea* and *The Tenth Power*, as well as a stand-alone Tremaris novel, *The Taste of Lightning*. She has also written two novels in the Girlfriend Fiction series, *Always Mackenzie* and *Winter of Grace*. Kate lives in Melbourne with her husband and two daughters.